全民英檢學習指南
中級聽讀測驗

The Official Preparation Guide to the
GEPT Intermediate Level Test

LTTC® 財團 語言訓練測驗中心
法人
THE LANGUAGE TRAINING & TESTING CENTER

前言

　　「全民英檢」（GEPT）分級標準參考我國學制與教育部英語課程綱要，題型與命題內容符合各階段英語學習者的特質與需要。GEPT 自 2000 年推出至今，持續進行信效度研究，精進測驗品質。自 2021 年 1 月起，GEPT 調整初、中、中高級聽讀測驗的題型與內容，並提供成績回饋服務，另，旨在反映 108 國教新課綱以「素養」為核心的教育理念與「學習導向評量（Learning Oriented Assessment）」的精神，期透過適當的測驗內容與成績回饋，更有效地促進學習，提升國人英語溝通力。

　　題型調整後，GEPT 內容將更貼近日常生活，且更符合我國各階段英語學習的歷程，例如：納入更多元的體裁和文本，評量真實生活、校園與職場情境下英語溝通及解決問題的能力。

　　為幫助學習者熟悉題型調整後 GEPT 的測驗內容與題型，降低實際測驗時的焦慮感，並培養正確的英語學習方法與策略，本中心特別編製《全民英檢學習指南》系列。有別於市面上著重於應試技巧的測驗準備書籍，本書以學習為導向，並融入培養核心素養的學習建議，期盼學習者除了持續累積英語實力外，亦能培養統整歸納與反思評鑑等關鍵思辯能力。

　　本中心期許《全民英檢學習指南》能正向強化讀者的學習動機，培養積極的學習態度。不論是準備全民英檢的學習者，報考會考、指考、學測的學生或是希望加強英語能力的自學者，皆可藉本書的試題檢視自己聽解與閱讀能力的強弱項，並配合書中的學習建議持續練習，我們相信學習者定能精進英語實力。

執行長 沈冬

財團法人語言訓練測驗中心

CONTENTS

全民英檢學習指南—中級聽讀測驗

導讀

　　本書是專為英語程度 CEFR B1 學習者設計的學習指南，可以做為準備學測、指考、與全民英檢中級使用，也適合自修、練習使用。本書分兩部份，第一部份為聽力閱讀練習題，第二部份為學習指南。練習題依照全民英檢正式測驗規格編寫，難易度、長度等都與正式測驗相同，測驗的設計以學習為導向，並融入核心素養，鼓勵自主學習，幫助學習者強化英文實力。學習指南內容包括：

1. 題型說明：簡介題型與評量的能力

2. 考前提醒：提示評量重點、題型與應答要訣

3. 試題解析：詳解題目與選項；2021 年起調整的題型以 New! 標記

4. 關鍵字詞：提供關鍵字釋義、例句與延伸學習

5. 學習策略：加強聽解、閱讀能力與相關核心素養的學習方法與策略

針對閱讀理解題的長篇文章，進一步提供：

6. 文本分析：解析文章的架構，說明每段的主旨與內容

7. 延伸思考：深化對文章主題的理解，提供延伸思考題，鍛鍊系統性思考與解決問題的核心素養

使用說明

步驟一 練習限時作答聽力閱讀練習題。

    ✓ 請搭配隨附 MP3 光碟或掃描 QR code 聆聽聽力音檔,並依照規定的作答時間作答。

    ✓ 作答完畢後,請核對答案。

    ✓ 檢視自己答錯的題目,聽力部份可對照錄音稿確認自己沒聽懂的關鍵訊息,閱讀部份則再仔細閱讀一次文本。

步驟二 研讀學習指南。

    ✓ 先看題型說明與考前提醒,了解各題型可運用的策略與注意事項,想想看有哪些策略是自己忽略的,並練習運用在答題。

    ✓ 閱讀試題解析,特別留意自己答錯的題目需運用的能力,再加強自己的弱項。

    ✓ 閱讀文本分析,了解長篇文章的架構與脈絡,幫助進一步理解文章內容。

    ✓ 閱讀關鍵字詞,透過所提供的例句,學習如何靈活運用相關詞彙。

    ✓ 查閱延伸思考,透過本書提供的思考問題加深對該議題的理解,並培養批判性思考。

    ✓ 最後讀學習策略所提供的建議,持續累積實力。

中級聽力與閱讀測驗簡介

中級 聽力測驗

時間	部份	題型	題數	總題數
約 30 分鐘	一	看圖辨義	5	35
	二	問答	10	
	三	簡短對話	10	
	四	簡短談話	10	

中級 閱讀測驗

時間	部份	題型	題數	總題數
45 分鐘	一	詞彙	10	35
	二	段落填空	10	
	三	閱讀理解	15	

能力說明

具有使用簡單英語進行日常生活溝通的能力。

聽力

能聽懂與日常或校園生活、工作相關的會話與談話、公共場所廣播、電視／廣播節目、氣象預報、廣告、簡易的操作說明等。

通過中級的英語學習者能理解日常生活中朋友、家人、陌生人間,互動和交換資訊的談話,並且能明確指出談話裡關於時間、地點等資訊的內容;能掌握主旨大意、說話者的態度、意見等。能聽懂日常生活中的電話留言、公共場所廣播、主題熟悉的電視廣告、新聞報導或廣播節目。能掌握學術與職場上架構清楚的簡短演說和簡易的操作指示。

能讀懂平鋪直敘，主題熟悉的短文，例如個人或正式信件、公告、新聞等應用文與說明文。

通過中級的英語學習者能讀懂日常生活中簡單的短文，並充分掌握描述人、事、時、地、物等資訊；能因應不同閱讀任務需求，整合歸納文章中的訊息，辨識文章大意、推測作者的態度、立場等。日常生活中，能讀懂個人書信、公共場所的標語、公告等。充分掌握主題熟悉的報章雜誌內容，和學術與職場上簡易的文件。

閱讀

通過標準

級數	測驗項目	通過標準
中級	聽力測驗 閱讀測驗	兩項測驗成績總和達 160 分，且其中任一項成績不低於 72 分。

Note

練習題

中級聽力測驗

掃描 QR Code
聆聽音檔

本測驗分四部份，全為四選一之選擇題，共 35 題，作答時間約 30 分鐘。

第一部份：看圖辨義

共 5 題，試題冊上有數幅圖畫，每一圖畫有 1~3 個描述該圖的題目，每題請聽光碟放音機播出題目以及四個英語敘述之後，選出與所看到的圖畫最相符的答案，每題只播出一遍。

例：（看）

Julie　　　Tom　　　Jane

（聽）　Look at the picture. Who is taller?

A. Julie is taller than Tom.
B. Tom is taller than Julie.
C. Jane is taller than Tom.
D. Julie is taller than Jane.

正確答案為 B。

GEPT®

L   L   L   L   L

聽力測驗第一部份試題自本頁開始。

A.　<u>Question 1</u>

B.　<u>Question 2</u>

Please turn to the next page. ▶

C. <u>Questions 3 and 4</u>

Great bargains!

Used furniture, tools, clothing, etc.
All items in good condition!

Date: Sat., September 3
Time: 9:00 - 15:00
Address: 20 Walker Road

D. <u>Question 5</u>

Students' Hobbies

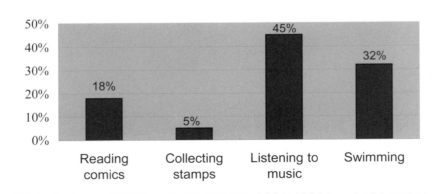

L L L L L

第二部份：問答
共 10 題，每題請聽光碟放音機播出一英語問句或直述句之後，從試題冊上 A、B、C、D 四個回答或回應中，選出一個最適合者作答。每題只播出一遍。

例： （聽） Since we're in Hualien, let's go to Taroko Gorge and enjoy the sights.
（看） A. You can practice English with them.
　　　 B. Yes. I'm on the road to recovery.
　　　 C. O.K. That sounds like fun.
　　　 D. An hour on foot from here.

正確答案為 C。

Please turn to the next page. ❯

6. A. I felt relieved that you were safe.
    B. I can never thank you enough.
    C. I usually get ready beforehand.
    D. I thought you already knew.

7. A. Yes. Could I have the menu again?
    B. Can I help you with something?
    C. Have you been here before?
    D. No. I'm sure no one has ever done it.

8. A. Yes. I see what you mean.
    B. Yes. I spoke with him earlier.
    C. No. I must not have seen it.
    D. No. I didn't bring it with me.

9. A. This way, please.
    B. Close to the suburbs, I guess.
    C. It's the biggest in the world.
    D. Just a ten-minute walk.

10. A. No wonder. He's very lucky.
    B. Indeed. He's spent a lot of time on it.
    C. Not at all. You're so kind.
    D. Count me in. I'd love to come along.

11. A. So soon? It's only 10:00.
    B. Yes, I think she enjoyed it.
    C. I'm so happy you'll be able to come.
    D. That's too bad. I'm busy that evening.

12. A. He must've offended her.
    B. You're not in charge, are you?
    C. I missed his call.
    D. Did she look convinced?

13. A. Yes. My train was 15 minutes late.
    B. Maybe not. There was a long line.
    C. OK. I bought four front seats.
    D. No. Everything was perfect.

14. A. Yes. I'll go to the open house.
    B. Yes. Their equipment is first class.
    C. Yes. That pair fits him very well.
    D. Yes. You have to take a shower first.

15. A. Can I put it on?
    B. I'll take a chance.
    C. You can use mine.
    D. Will you sponsor me?

L   L   L   L   L

第三部份：簡短對話

共 10 題，每題請聽光碟放音機播出一段對話及一個相關的問題後，從
試題冊上 A、B、C、D 四個選項中選出一個最適合者作答。每段對話
及問題只播出一遍。

例：　（聽）　(Woman)　Good morning. Is this the platform for the train to Min-Hsiung?
　　　　　　(Man)　　No. Only express trains stop here. The train you want is a local,
　　　　　　　　　　　and it stops on platform 3.
　　　　　　(Woman)　I see. I must've gone in the wrong direction. I've never
　　　　　　　　　　　actually taken a train from here before.

　　　　　　Question:　Why does the woman need the man's help?

　　（看）　　A.　She can't find her ticket.
　　　　　　　B.　She's not familiar with the station.
　　　　　　　C.　She boarded the wrong train.
　　　　　　　D.　She missed her stop.

正確答案為 B。

16. A. A successful chain of theaters.
    B. A trend in the entertainment
       industry.
    C. The director of a classic film.
    D. General opinion about an actor.

17. A. He can't find the file he needs.
    B. He'll be away from his office.
    C. He was interrupted by someone.
    D. He has to reply to an email first.

18. A. Their family members.
    B. The fast pace of their lives.
    C. Their next destination.
    D. The terrible traffic.

19. A. A sense of humor.
    B. A desire to succeed.
    C. An appreciation of art.
    D. An instinct for survival.

20. A. She's a photographer.
    B. She's a businesswoman.
    C. She's a reporter.
    D. She's a teacher.

21. A. File a complaint about a plumber.
    B. Hire an experienced plumber.
    C. Borrow some plumbing tools.
    D. Learn more plumbing skills.

22. A. A traditional dish.
    B. A holiday custom.
    C. A planned trip to China.
    D. New numbers for his door.

23. A. A booklet.
    B. A receipt.
    C. A bill.
    D. A ticket.

24. Kelly's Red Envelope Money ($30,000)

    A. Buying a cell phone.
    B. Getting new clothes.
    C. Donating to charity.
    D. Saving in the bank.

25.

NOTES
▪ Grand Hotel: Gym and pool
▪ Express Inn: Shuttle to and from airport
▪ Days Hotel: 5-min walk to attractions
▪ Soho B&B: Low room rates

    A. Grand Hotel.
    B. Express Inn.
    C. Days Hotel.
    D. Soho B&B.

L L L L L

共 10 題，每題請聽光碟放音機播出一段談話及一個相關的問題後，從試題冊上 A、B、C、D 四個選項中選出一個最適合者作答。每段談話及問題只播出一遍。

例： （聽） Everyone, please complete the registration form first. If you've never taken a class here before, you'll also need to present your ID, provide two photos, and pay $100 so that the staff can create a student card for you. But if you've been a student here before, the photos and registration fee are not necessary. Just inform the office staff when you submit your registration.

Question:　　What should a returning student do to register?

（看） A.　Provide two photos.
　　　 B.　Fill out a form.
　　　 C.　Show their ID card.
　　　 D.　Pay the registration fee.

正確答案為 B。

26. A. To offer an apology.
    B. To give advice.
    C. To show admiration.
    D. To express concern.

27. A. By buying more than twenty items.
    B. By shopping with a friend.
    C. By making a purchase early.
    D. By ordering something online.

28. A. Why children will love it.
    B. Which teams will show up.
    C. What benefits it may bring.
    D. How people can sign up.

29. A. Her nervous feelings.
    B. The response from her audience.
    C. A short story she told.
    D. A device problem.

30. A. Self-defense.
    B. Rock climbing.
    C. Dancing.
    D. Soccer.

31. A. In an aquarium.
    B. In a zoo.
    C. On a farm.
    D. At a playground.

32. A. Solutions to it.
    B. Public attitudes to it.
    C. The business opportunities.
    D. The important causes.

33. A. It's not unusual.
    B. It should be evaluated.
    C. It's quite welcome.
    D. It won't have an impact.

34.

Participant: Emily Huang	
Judge	Score given
Tim Wilson	91
Hugo Davis	95
Frank Taylor	88
Peter Carter	70

    A. Tim Wilson.
    B. Hugo Davis.
    C. Frank Taylor.
    D. Peter Carter.

35.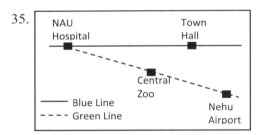

    A. NAU Hospital Station.
    B. Nehu Airport Station.
    C. Central Zoo Station.
    D. Town Hall Station.

– 結束 –

R　　R　　R　　R　　R

閱讀能力測驗

　　本測驗分三部份，全為四選一之選擇題，共 35 題，作答時間 45 分鐘。

第一部份：詞彙
　　　　共 10 題，每題含一個空格。請由試題冊上的四個選項中選出最適合題
　　　　意的字或詞作答。

Please turn to the next page. ❯

R R R R R

1. The firefighters are trying to _____ the boy who is trapped in the house that is on fire.
   A. rescue
   B. defeat
   C. propose
   D. illustrate

2. The nurse will take the patient's blood pressure again because the first reading did not seem to be _____.
   A. durable
   B. permanent
   C. conservative
   D. accurate

3. Dressing _____ is a simple but effective way to make a favorable initial impression.
   A. clumsily
   B. properly
   C. hurriedly
   D. beneficially

4. Mom often divides household _____, such as doing the dishes or taking out the trash, among my brothers and me.
   A. goods
   B. expenses
   C. chores
   D. appliances

5. After _____ the dust that had long covered the old photograph, Jack was finally able to identify the people in it.
   A. handing over
   B. wiping away
   C. snapping off
   D. rising up

6. In order to better manage his allowance, Scott has decided to record his daily expenses _____.
   A. in return
   B. back and forth
   C. from now on
   D. behind the times

7. Steve's desire to play on the school basketball team has _____ him to practice every day.
   A. explored
   B. motivated
   C. composed
   D. organized

8. The _____ for Sandy's business trip will be arranged by her company.
   A. accommodation
   B. representation
   C. inspiration
   D. expectation

9. If you want to write a good science paper, you must provide enough _____ and use it effectively to support your argument.
   A. significance
   B. occupation
   C. endurance
   D. evidence

10. Do not skip meals anymore; _____ eating may harm your stomach.
    A. practical
    B. vegetarian
    C. irregular
    D. essential

R R R R R

第二部份：段落填空

共 10 題，包括二個段落，每個段落各含 5 個空格。請由試題冊上四個
選項中選出最適合題意的字或詞作答。

Questions 11-15

Jason had imagined himself going skydiving ever since he was a child. Last
Saturday, for his twentieth birthday, he finally __(11)__. His parents generously paid for
him to take lessons from a qualified __(12)__, Sherry Black. On the morning of Jason's
birthday, Sherry introduced to Jason the equipment they needed and explained the best
way to use it. She then __(13)__ how to jump out of the plane and land safely. After lunch,
she and Jason went up in a small plane __(14)__ a pilot. When they reached a height of
4,000 meters, Sherry and Jason jumped out of the plane and then quickly opened their
parachutes. __(15)__, they drifted slowly to the ground. Jason had a wonderful time and
is looking forward to a new adventure on his next birthday.

11. A. experienced what it was really
       like
    B. invited his friends to his birthday
       party
    C. had the courage to ask a girl out
    D. got his license to fly an airplane

12. A. spectator
    B. ambassador
    C. instructor
    D. competitor

13. A. implemented
    B. demonstrated
    C. expanded
    D. attempted

14. A. with
    B. to
    C. of
    D. upon

15. A. Nevertheless
    B. At first
    C. Particularly
    D. After that

R R R R R

Questions 16-20

Certain high-pitched sounds can be heard by youngsters but not by adults. An inventor in England has applied this knowledge to a device called the Mosquito, which is intended to keep young trouble-makers away from stores by __(16)__. Some shops in England have complained about the __(17)__ behavior of teenage gangs who gather nearby and scare customers away. One solution to this problem is to __(18)__ a Mosquito near the front door. __(19)__ teenage gangs come around, the painful sound the machine makes will force them to leave. Of course, the Mosquito may also __(20)__ other young customers. But this isn't a serious problem for shops that mainly sell products to adults.

16. A. producing an awful buzz
    B. putting up a warning sign
    C. sprinkling water on them
    D. releasing harmful insects

17. A. competitive
    B. annoying
    C. responsible
    D. forgetful

18. A. access
    B. observe
    C. install
    D. affect

19. A. As soon as
    B. Even so
    C. Unless
    D. Despite

20. A. tolerate
    B. discourage
    C. withdraw
    D. remove

R R R R R

共 15 題，包括 5 個題組，每個題組含 1 至 2 篇短文，與數個相關的四選一的選擇題。請由試題冊上的選項中選出最適合者作答。

Questions 21-22

Underwater World

On Fisherman Road next to Civic Harbor

Are you ready for a close encounter with sharks, jellyfish, and giant turtles?

Visit *Underwater World*, home of the nation's largest exhibits of ocean life, and you will see sea creatures you have never seen before as you walk through our 100-meter-long glass tunnel.

Do not miss our daily seal shows, which start at 11:00 A.M. and 2:00 P.M.

Opening hours:

Monday to Saturday, 10:00 A.M. to 8:00 P.M.

Sunday, 10:00 A.M. to 5:00 P.M.

Entrance fees:

Children aged 6 and under: Free

Students: NT$250

Adults: NT$400

Senior citizens (over 65): NT$200

21. What is this advertisement for?
    A. A huge aquarium
    B. A fishing trip
    C. A famous museum
    D. An underground mall

22. What information can be found in the advertisement?
    A. How to make a reservation
    B. What kind of seafood is served
    C. How long the show will last
    D. Who needs to pay for a ticket

Questions 23-25

From:	martinK@netmail.com
To:	kph97@mail.com
Subject:	Greetings

Dear Kim,

Thank you for the postcard. That was very sweet. I miss you very much, too, and I'm glad to know that your summer job at your uncle's hotel is going well.

Well, my parents finally agreed to let me buy a motorcycle. My dad suggested that I get an electric one and promised to share the cost. After looking at many models, I chose one last week. It's very quiet and makes less pollution than a gasoline-powered one.

Now that I have my own vehicle, I want to visit you. According to my map, Fantasy Lake is only a few miles from your uncle's hotel. I would like to go fishing there and stay at your uncle's hotel for one night. Let me know your days off.

Take care, and write back soon.

Regards,
Martin

23. What is true about Martin and Kim's relationship?
    A. They were schoolmates who founded a club.
    B. They are friends who have not met for some time.
    C. They are neighbors who are preparing an activity.
    D. They were colleagues who worked closely together.

24. What can be learned about Martin's new motorcycle?
    A. It is environmentally friendly.
    B. It has a powerful engine.
    C. It has a striking appearance.
    D. It is custom-made.

25. Why does Martin hope to hear from Kim soon?
    A. He is seeking employment.
    B. He is sending Kim a present.
    C. He is asking Kim for help.
    D. He is planning a journey.

Questions 26-28

East Asians are familiar with the physical benefits of bathing in hot springs. In Finland, people use saunas for similar reasons. A sauna is a small wooden hut or a room inside a house. By means of a stove, the sauna is first heated to between seventy-one and one hundred degrees Celsius. After people shower and clean themselves, they go into the sauna and sit on a wooden bench. They take a towel with them to sit on, as the bench might be quite hot. Every few minutes, they pour some water over heated stones on top of the stove to create new steam. After a while they go outside, jump into a pond or take a cold shower, and then go back into the sauna again. They repeat this process two or three times and wash themselves again at the end. Afterwards, they enjoy Finnish sausage with beer or soft drinks. Saunas are very popular in Finland, and there are two million saunas for the country's entire population of 5.5 million people.

26. What is this article mainly about?
    A. How hot springs and saunas are different
    B. Why taking a sauna bath is good for you
    C. How people in Finland take a sauna bath
    D. Where the best locations for saunas are

27. Why do Finnish people take a towel with them into a sauna?
    A. To clean their faces when they sweat
    B. To protect themselves from getting burned
    C. To wrap their hair after a cold shower
    D. To dry the bench before sitting on it

28. What information is provided in the article?
    A. What people do after taking a sauna bath
    B. How many families have their own sauna
    C. Where people can find stones for the saunas
    D. When saunas were first built in Finland

Please turn to the next page. ❯

Questions 29-31 are based on the information provided in the following web page and email.

Roommate Wanted

Two English majors at Springfield University are looking for someone to share a comfortable, three-bedroom apartment within easy walking distance of the campus. The room will be vacant after July 25. To sharpen our English skills, we enforce a strict "English only" policy in the house. For this reason, we prefer applicants whose mother tongue is English. We also need someone who can pay rent on time and share the housework. If you are interested, please contact Phil at <u>aming@uni. edu.tw</u>. For pictures of the apartment, click **here**.

R R R R R

From: bsmith@uni.edu.tw

To: aming@uni.edu.tw

Subject: Room for rent

Hi Phil,

I am writing in response to your "Roommate Wanted" post. I'm very interested in this apartment since the location is perfect for me. It's near a night market, and I also study at Springfield University. You stated you prefer native English speakers. I am an exchange student from Australia, and am certain I could help you improve your English. I am an easy-going person, and I like to keep my living space tidy and clean. In your pictures, I saw gym equipment, which would be good for my new workout routine. Your cat also looks very cute! I only have one question. My summer program will start on July 1, so I'd like to know if it's possible for me to move in before then. Looking forward to hearing from you!

Cheers,
Brandon Smith

29. Which aspect of a potential roommate does the notice emphasize?
    A. Their major in college
    B. Their gender
    C. Their hobby
    D. Their first language

30. What do we know about Phil?
    A. He hopes to adopt a pet.
    B. He goes to the gym every morning.
    C. He lives near a night market.
    D. He speaks Mandarin with his roommates.

31. If Phil rejects Brandon, what might be the reason?
    A. Brandon is difficult to get along with.
    B. The rent Brandon suggests is too low.
    C. He has nothing in common with Brandon.
    D. The date Brandon needs to move in is too early.

R R R R R

請翻頁作答第 32-35 題

Questions 32-35

In the 1730s, America consisted of thirteen English colonies, one of which was New York. The governor of New York, William Cosby, was appointed to his position by the English government. He was widely disliked because of his attempts to raise his own salary, seize lands, and even influence the result of a local election.

In 1733, a newspaper published articles that described Cosby's abuses of power. In response, Cosby had the publisher, John Peter Zenger, arrested and put in jail. Zenger was accused of damaging Cosby's reputation by making false statements about him.

Zenger spent eight months in prison before appearing in court. Two judges and a twelve-man jury listened to the case. Zenger's lawyer admitted that Zenger had printed the articles about Cosby. However, he fiercely defended Zenger's right as a journalist to tell the truth about people even if it disgraced them.

After discussing the case, the jury ruled in favor of Zenger, saying that he had not committed any crime because what he had published could be proven. As a result, Zenger was set free. It was the first trial in America that focused on a newspaper's right to publish articles critical of government officials or other people. The ruling helped to establish the principle of freedom of the press, a right that journalists in America and many other countries enjoy today.

32. What is the main subject of this article?
    A. An election with opposing candidates
    B. A debate between rival newspapers
    C. A false statement about an official
    D. A legal case involving a journalist

33. What was the public's opinion of Cosby?
    A. His experience was inadequate.
    B. He would improve in time.
    C. His conduct was wrong.
    D. He deserved a higher salary.

34. What was the intention of Cosby's action towards Zenger?
    A. To stop attacks against Zenger
    B. To persuade Zenger to leave the U.S.
    C. To release Zenger from prison
    D. To destroy Zenger's career

35. What was the final decision about Zenger?
    A. His demands were not realistic.
    B. He was found innocent.
    C. He received a light punishment.
    D. His property would be seized.

－ 結 束 －

聽力與閱讀測驗解答

聽力測驗解答

第一部份		第二部份		第三部份		第四部份	
題 號	正 答	題 號	正 答	題 號	正 答	題 號	正 答
1	C	6	D	16	D	26	D
2	A	7	A	17	C	27	C
3	C	8	B	18	B	28	C
4	D	9	B	19	A	29	D
5	B	10	B	20	C	30	A
		11	A	21	B	31	C
		12	A	22	B	32	A
		13	D	23	A	33	C
		14	B	24	D	34	D
		15	C	25	C	35	D

閱讀能力測驗解答

第一部份		第二部份		第三部份	
題 號	正 答	題 號	正 答	題 號	正 答
1	A	11	A	21	A
2	D	12	C	22	D
3	B	13	B	23	B
4	C	14	A	24	A
5	B	15	D	25	D
6	C	16	A	26	C
7	B	17	B	27	B
8	A	18	C	28	A
9	D	19	A	29	D
10	C	20	B	30	C
				31	D
				32	D
				33	C
				34	D
				35	B

※「全民英檢」中級聽力、閱讀測驗採電腦閱卷，滿分120分。聽力測驗每題3.4分，閱讀測驗每題3.4分。為使歷次測驗的成績可以直接進行比較，考生成績將根據粗分（答對題數乘以每題分數）透過統計方式調整，以維持測驗成績的可比性。

聽力測驗錄音內容

測驗即將開始，如果音量太大或太小，請舉手告訴監試人員。

The test is about to begin. If you have any problem with the volume of the recording, please raise your hand now.

全民英語能力分級檢定測驗

中級聽力測驗

本測驗分四部份，全為四選一之選擇題，共 35 題，作答時間約 30 分鐘。

第一部份：看圖辨義

共 5 題，試題冊上有數幅圖畫，每一圖畫有 1 ～ 3 個描述該圖的題目，每題請聽光碟放音機播出題目以及四個英語敘述之後，選出與所看到的圖畫最相符的答案，每題只播出一遍。

請看例圖

請聽例題： Look at the picture. Who is taller?
A. Julie is taller than Tom.
B. Tom is taller than Julie.
C. Jane is taller than Tom.
D. Julie is taller than Jane.

正確答案為 B。

測驗即將開始，如果音量太大或太小，請舉手告訴監試人員。

The test is about to begin. If you have any problem with the volume of the recording, please raise your hand now.

現在請翻開試題冊。

現在開始聽力測驗第一部份。

For question number 1, please look at picture A.

Question number 1: Where are these people?

A. In a clinic.

B. In a laboratory.

C. In an art gallery.

D. In a travel agency.

For question number 2, please look at picture B.

Question number 2: What might the woman be saying?

A.   I'm afraid we'll have to cancel the picnic.

B. Could you make a copy of this report?

C. I asked for French fries with that!

D. The sky looks really clear!

For questions number 3 and 4, please look at picture C.

Question number 3: Who might be interested in this advertisement?

A. People who love indoor activities.

B. People who are looking for a friendly roommate.

C. People who want to shop for second-hand household items.

D. People who are looking for a convenient place to live.

Question number 4: Please look at picture C again. What information is provided in the
advertisement?

A. The cost.

B. The phone number.

C. The name of the owner.

D. The location.

For question number 5, please look at picture D.

Question number 5: According to this chart, what do we know about students' hobbies?

A.   Over half of the students like to listen to music.

B. Nearly one third of the students enjoy swimming.

C. More students collect stamps than read comics.

D. Swimming is the most common hobby among the students.

第二部份：問答

共 10 題，每題請聽光碟放音機播出一英語問句或直述句之後，從試題冊上 A、B、C、D 四個回答或回應中，選出一個最適合者作答。每題只播出一遍。

請聽例題： Since we're in Hualien, let's go to Taroko Gorge and enjoy the sights.

請看選項： A. You can practice English with them.
B. Yes. I'm on the road to recovery.
C. O.K. That sounds like fun.
D. An hour on foot from here.

正確答案為 C。

現在開始聽力測驗第二部份。

6. Why didn't you tell me earlier? There's nothing I can do now.

7. Would you care for some dessert?

8. Did you ask your teacher for the day off tomorrow?

9. In which part of the city will the amusement park be built?

10. Jack showed me his coin collection the other day. It was amazing.

11. It was a wonderful party, Sue, but we really must be going.

12. Nicole is still angry with George for what he said the other day.

13. Susan, how was the concert last night? I heard it was delayed.

14. Have you been to the gym at the new community sports center yet?

15. If I had known it would be such a sunny day, I would've brought my suntan lotion.

　　　　共 10 題，每題請聽光碟放音機播出一段對話及一個相關的問題後，從試題冊上 A、B、C、D 四個選項中選出一個最適合者作答。每段對話及問題只播出一遍。

請聽例題：　(Woman)　Good morning. Is this the platform for the train to Min-Hsiung?

(Man)　No. Only express trains stop here. The train you want is a local, and it stops on platform 3.

(Woman)　I see. I must've gone in the wrong direction. I've never actually taken a train from here before.

Question: Why does the woman need the man's help?

請看選項：　A. She can't find her ticket.
B. She's not familiar with the station.
C. She boarded the wrong train.
D. She missed her stop.

正確答案為 B。

現在開始聽力測驗第三部份。

16. M: Who's that on the cover of your magazine?
　　W: Richard Howard. He's starred in several movies lately. Have you seen any of them?
　　M: No, but I've heard good things about him.
　　W: Actually, quite a few people think he's handsome but has little talent.
　　M: Oh? I'm surprised to hear that.

Question: What is the main subject of this conversation?

Please turn to the next page.

17. W: Hello? Accounting Division.

 M: Hello, Diane. It's Jack. I have a question for you.

 W: Certainly. What's up?

 M: I was looking at the proposal you gave me yesterday, and …. Oh, I'm sorry, Diane, someone just came into my office and I need to talk to her. Can I call you back?

 W: Sure. I'll be here at my desk.

 M: I'll call you back in a few minutes.

Question: Why will the man call the woman back?

18. M: Have you been busy recently?

 W: Too busy. With my new job, plus taking care of my kids and running errands, I feel like I'm always on the go. I'm exhausted.

 M: I know what you mean. Sometimes I wish the world would just slow down.

 W: I doubt that will ever happen.

Question: What are these people mainly discussing?

19. W: Everyone in our class seems to enjoy telling jokes.

 M: Yes, but I seldom find them to be very funny.

 W: I noticed that you don't laugh very much. Why are you so serious, Bill?

 M: I don't know. I guess it's just my personality.

Question: What does the man seem to lack?

20. M: Metropolitan Museum. How may I help you?
    W: Yes, I'm writing a short article about the Japanese art exhibition you're having next month. Can you tell me when it will start?
    M: July 3, and it runs for six weeks.
    W: I heard one of the artists is visiting Taiwan.
    M: Yes, and he'll attend the opening ceremony at 10 A.M. on the third.
    W: Good, that's all I need to know.
    M: Where will the article appear?
    W: In the *Daily Post*.

    Question: What does the woman do for a living?

21. W: Paul? One of the pipes under the kitchen sink is leaking.
    M: Again? I just fixed that a week ago.
    W: I know.
    M: I guess I'd better call Randy Robinson this time. He can do a better job of fixing it than I can.
    W: Does he do this kind of work for a living now?
    M: Yes, and his charges are reasonable.

    Question: What is the man planning to do this time?

22. M: What are those strips of paper you're putting on your door?
    W: These are for good luck.
    M: I've never seen anything like that before.
    W: We put up new ones at Chinese New Year and leave them on the door all year.
    M: Does everyone in your country do that?
    W: Not everyone does, but a lot of people do. It's a tradition.

    Question: What are the speakers talking about?

23. W: What are you looking for?

    M: The manual for this coffee machine. I can't remember how to use it.

    W: Is the manual small?

    M: Yes.

    W: Then check the cabinet in the study. I recently put some small manuals there.

    Question: What is the man looking for?

For question number 24, please look at the pie chart.

24. M: Kelly, what are you going to do with your red envelope this year?

    W: I'm going to spend all of it on a cell phone and some clothes.

    M: I think you should put half of the money in the bank and donate one-third like we did last year. And then you can spend the rest on shopping.

    W: That'll leave me…only five thousand dollars!

    M: That should be enough.

    W: All right, Dad.

    Question: Look at the pie chart. What does the area marked with a star refer to?

For question number 25, please look at the note.

25. W: Have you decided where we will stay in London?

    M: I've found a few nice hotels. Do we need to stay on a tight budget this trip?

    W: I think we can afford a little luxury. Are any of them convenient for getting to castles and art galleries in the downtown area?

    M: Hmm, neither the Express Inn nor the Grand Hotel is close to the city center.

    W: That's not ideal. Most places we want to visit are in the city center.

    M: I see. Now I know where we should stay.

    Question: Look at the note. Which hotel will the speakers most likely choose?

第四部份：簡短談話

共 10 題，每題請聽光碟放音機播出一段談話及一個相關的問題後，從試題冊上 A、B、C、D 四個選項中選出一個最適合者作答。每段談話及問題只播出一遍。

請聽例題： Everyone, please complete the registration form first. If you've never taken a class here before, you'll also need to present your ID, provide two photos, and pay $100 so that the staff can create a student card for you. But if you've been a student here before, the photos and registration fee are not necessary. Just inform the office staff when you submit your registration.

Question: What should a returning student do to register?

請看選項：
A. Provide two photos.
B. Fill out a form.
C. Show their ID card.
D. Pay the registration fee.

正確答案為 B。

現在開始聽力測驗第四部份。

26. Hello, Caroline. It's Henry. I talked to your mom earlier today, and she told me about the surgery. I've been really worried. I'll come to the hospital to see you sometime tomorrow. Just let me know if you need anything. Hope you get well soon!

Question: What is the purpose of this message?

27. The summer sale is coming! From August 13th to 19th, everything at Jerry's Stationery will be twenty percent off. A free notebook will be given to the first twenty shoppers. More amazing savings will be offered. Hurry up and visit us at 30 Pacific Avenue.

Question: According to the commercial, how will people get a free notebook?

28. In local news, basketball games for young children will be held at Forest Park this coming Saturday. The organizer of the games, the Southend Community Center, states that children who play team sports are healthier and have better social skills. By holding this event, the center hopes to encourage more children to take up sports.

Question: What is said about the event?

29. Our graduation program was held in the college gym. As class leader, I gave a speech. But two minutes after I began speaking, the microphone stopped working. The program director gave me another one, but it didn't work, either. In the end, I had to speak without a microphone. I don't think anyone beyond the third row could hear me.

Question: What is the woman saying about her speech?

30. Have you all found a partner? Good, let's practice some moves. One of you be the attacker, and the other be the victim. Attacker, grab hold of your partner's right arm. Now victim, turn around and kick your partner in the knee. Lightly, of course. In real situations, you will have to use as much force as you can.

Question: What is the speaker teaching?

31. Hi, I'm Nancy, and I'm your guide today. I'm going to take you through the entire area, so you'll be able to see all the animals that we raise, including horses, cows, chickens, and sheep. You'll also have the chance to milk a cow and gather the chickens' eggs. Many of our products, such as milk, cheese, and eggs, are sold at department stores. You can place an order at the end of the tour. Everyone ready to go?

Question: Where is the speaker?

32. The world is facing an environmental crisis that affects every living thing. Thankfully, there are things we can do to address the crisis. We can turn off the lights, avoid using the air conditioner, and take part in recycling projects. These three things can help to cut down the energy we consume. All it takes is a little effort on everyone's part.

Question: What aspect of the environmental crisis does the speaker focus on?

33. The teacher of my nine-year-old son, William, has a no-homework policy. This means that students are expected to finish their assignment during school hours. There's no extra work for them to bring home. Thanks to this policy, William has time for his hobbies, and we have more family time together.

Question: What would the speaker say about the teacher's homework policy?

For question number 34, please look at the score board.
34. I was a judge for the English Writing Contest this year. I was careful to follow the rating instructions, but later, when my scores were compared with those of the other three judges, there was a huge difference. For example, this year's champion is Emily Huang, but I wasn't impressed by her performance at all.

Question: Look at the score board. Who is the speaker?

For question number 35, please look at the route map.
35. Attention ladies and gentlemen. Due to mechanical problems, the Blue Line has suspended service. Passengers who wish to travel to stations on the Blue Line, please take the Green Line or alternative transportation. The City Subway System apologizes for the inconvenience.

Question: Look at the route map. Which station cannot be reached by subway now?

This is the end of the Listening Comprehension Test.

聽力測驗結束。

Note

學習指南

PICTURE
DESCRIPTION

中級聽力

第一部份

看圖辨義

聽力測驗 第一部份 看圖辨義

這個部份共 5 題，試題冊上有數幅圖畫，每一圖畫有 1-3 個描述該圖的題目，每題請聽題目以及四個英語敘述之後，選出與所看到的圖畫最相符的答案。

本部份評量的學習表現包括：

- ✓ 能聽懂日常生活用語與常用句型的句子
- ✓ 能聽懂人、事、時、地、物的描述及問答
- ✓ 能綜合相關資訊做合理的猜測

考前提醒

這個部份評量的是口語中常用的詞彙與句型，取材貼近日常生活，與生活經驗息息相關，例如描述地點、位置、動作、衣著、外表、天氣、食物、交通工具、嗜好等，符合素養導向強調的真實情境。平時只要多熟悉日常生活中常見的詞彙和句型即可輕鬆應答。

回答這類型的題目時

1. 首先快速瀏覽圖片，掌握情境

   聆聽題目之前先快速瀏覽圖片，掌握圖片所描繪的場景、人物或動作。例如第 **3-4** 題是一張廣告傳單，可以先瀏覽圖片中的時間、地點與販賣的物品等，才不會遺漏作答相關的訊息。

2. 看清楚圖表題的標題與符號

   如果不常接觸統計圖表，這類題目可能顯得陌生。但只要看清楚每個座標軸所代表的意義，仔細聆聽問題，對照問題與圖中的資訊，就可順利找到答案（例如第 **5** 題）。

3. 培養預測問題（prediction）的能力

   瀏覽圖片時可以一邊預測可能會出現的問題，同時整合聽到的相關線索，找出正確的答案。例如看到第 **1** 題的圖片時，可根據圖片的細節，推測問題可能會問圖片的地點或是圖片中的人在做什麼等。

熟悉這些作答策略，可以幫助你輕鬆應試！

第 1 題

Where are these people?　　　　這些人在哪裡？

A.　In a clinic.　　　　A.　在診所

B.　In a laboratory　　　　B.　在實驗室

C.　In an art gallery.　　　　C.　在藝廊

D.　In a travel agency.　　　　D.　在旅行社

正解 C

本題取材自生活場景，需根據圖片的資訊做合理的推測。由圖片看到：（1）這個空間裡展出畫作，（2）這些人正在欣賞作品。

題目問的是這些人在哪裡，由場景和圖片中人物的動作，我們可得知他們在藝廊或美術館欣賞畫作，故答案為 In an art gallery（在藝廊）。

關鍵字詞 art gallery 藝廊

B. 第 2 題

第 2 題

What might the woman be saying?

A. I'm afraid we'll have to cancel the picnic.

B. Could you make a copy of this report?

C. I asked for French fries with that!

D. The sky looks really clear!

女生可能正在說什麼？

A. 我們恐怕要取消野餐了。

B. 你可以複印這份報告嗎？

C. 我配菜點的是薯條！

D. 天空看起來很晴朗！

 正解 Ⓐ

本題取材自生活場景，需根據圖片的資訊做合理的推測。

圖片中的女子拉開窗簾，發現窗外下著大雨，我們可因此推測她可能會說和天氣相關的事情。選項 B、C 和本題情境不符，選項 D：The sky looks really clear!（天空看起來很晴朗）明顯和圖片所描繪的景象相反，只有選項 A：I'm afraid we'll have to cancel the picnic.（我們恐怕要取消野餐了）最為合理。因為野餐為戶外活動，天氣好壞會影響到活動進行，故本題答案為 A。

關鍵字詞 cancel 取消　picnic 野餐　clear 晴朗的、清楚的

Great bargains!

Used furniture, tools, clothing, etc.
All items in good condition!

Date: Sat., September 3
Time: 9:00 – 15:00
Address: 20 Walker Road

特賣會！

二手家具、工具、衣物等
全部商品保存良好！

日期： 9月3日禮拜六
時間： 9:00 – 15:00
地址： Walker路20號

第 3 題

Who might be interested in this advertisement?

A. People who love indoor activities.

B. People who are looking for a friendly roommate.

C. People who want to shop for second-hand household items.

D. People who are looking for a convenient place to live.

誰會對這則廣告有興趣？

A. 喜歡室內活動的人

B. 尋找友善室友的人

C. 想要買二手家用品的人

D. 尋找生活機能完善的住處的人

正解 C

本題取材自常見的廣告傳單，需從傳單的內容推論出相關資訊。

從傳單中的 bargain（特賣）、used furniture、tools、clothing（二手家具、工具、衣物），我們可得知這張傳單可能來自賣舊物的二手商店，因此本題正確答案是 C：People who want to shop for second-hand household items.（想要買二手家用品的人），其他選項的敘述都不符合傳單內容。

關鍵字詞 bargain 特價品、便宜貨 used 舊的、二手的 furniture 家具

第 4 題

Please look at picture C again. What information is provided in the advertisement?

A. The cost.

B. The phone number.

C. The name of the owner.

D. The location.

請再看一次圖片 C。廣告裡提供了什麼資訊？

A. 價格

B. 電話號碼

C. 老闆的姓名

D. 地點

正解 D

本題需對照傳單的細部資訊並仔細聆聽題目，才能選出正確答案。

從傳單中出現的 date（日期）、time（時間）、address（地址），我們可得知這間二手商店將在 9 月 3 日舉辦特賣會，地點在 Walker 路 20 號，因此本題正確答案是 D：The location（地點）。其他的選項如商品價格（cost）、電話號碼（phone number）、商店老闆的姓名（name of the owner）傳單裡面都沒有出現。

關鍵字詞 address 地址　location 地點、位置

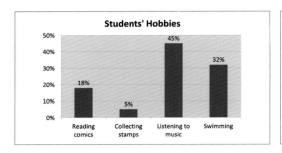

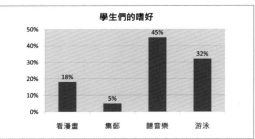

第 5 題

According to this chart, what do we know about students' hobbies?

A. Over half of the students like to listen to music.

B. Nearly one third of the students enjoy swimming.

C. More students collect stamps than read comics.

D. Swimming is the most common hobby among the students.

根據這張圖表，我們對學生的嗜好有何瞭解？

A. 超過半數的學生喜歡聽音樂。

B. 將近三分之一的學生喜歡游泳。

C. 收集郵票的學生多於看漫畫的學生。

D. 游泳是學生最普遍的嗜好。

正解 Ⓑ

本題取材自校園情境，圖表的內容是調查學生嗜好的結果。這類的圖表題其實不複雜，作答之前，先仔細閱讀圖表縱軸和橫軸的資訊，透過比較分析，歸納出答案。

以此題為例，縱軸顯示的是百分比（從事不同嗜好的學生人數比例），而橫軸列出的是項目（學生嗜好的種類）。綜合縱軸和橫軸的資訊判斷各個選項是否正確。由圖表可知，喜歡聽音樂的學生佔 45%，並未超過半數，因此選項 A 不正確。選項 B：Nearly one third of the students enjoy swimming.（將近三分之一的學生喜歡游泳。）符合圖表的描述，因此為正確答案。喜歡收集郵票的學生僅有 5%，並未超過喜歡看漫畫的學生（18%），故選項 C 也不是正確答案。另外，最多人喜歡的嗜好為聽音樂，因此 D 不是正確答案。

關鍵字詞 half 一半 one third 三分之一

💬 關鍵字詞

接著我們來複習本部份的重點詞彙

art gallery 藝廊（第 1 題）

例句 • An exhibition of paintings from the Renaissance period will be held at the art gallery in December.
在十二月，這間藝廊會舉辦一場文藝復興時期畫作的展覽。

cancel 動 取消（第 2 題）

例句 • I'm afraid we'll have to cancel the picnic.
我們恐怕要取消野餐了。

• Remind me to cancel my subscription to the gym next month since I'll be out of town for two weeks.
我即將要出遠門兩個禮拜，記得提醒我取消下個月健身房的會員。

picnic 名 野餐（第 2 題）

例句 • Our family used to go on a picnic at the lake together every summer when living in Hualien.
以前住在花蓮時，我們家族每年夏天都會去湖邊野餐。

clear 形 晴朗的、清楚的（第 2 題）

例句 • The sky looks really clear!
天空看起來很晴朗！

• We got a clear view of the mountains from the airplane.
我們在飛機上很清楚地看到山脈。

bargain 名 特價品、便宜貨（第 3 題）

例句 • The next time you go to Third Avenue, don't forget to check out the bargains in that supermarket on the corner.
下次你去第三大道時，別忘了去看一下角落那家超市的特價品。

延伸學習　What a bargain! 好划算！

used **形** 舊的、二手的 （第 3 題）

例句 • If you have budget issues, why not buy some used textbooks? Many of them are as good as new.
如果你有預算上的考量，何不買二手教科書呢？它們很多都像新的一樣。

furniture **名** 家具 （第 3 題）

例句 • I picked some second-hand furniture for my new apartment at a garage sale.
我在車庫舊物拍賣中買了一些二手家具放在我的新公寓。

address **名** 地址 （第 4 題）

例句 • The address you wrote on the envelope is in America, so you'll have to stick a twenty-eight-dollar stamp on it.
你信封上的地址寫的是美國，所以你要貼二十八元的郵票。

location **名** 地點、位置 （第 4 題）

例句 • The app on your smartphone enables you to check your location at any time.
你智慧型手機上的那個軟體可以讓你隨時查看你目前的位置。

half **名** 一半 （第 5 題）

例句 • Over half of the students like to listen to music.
超過半數的學生喜歡聽音樂。

• Half of the audience asked for a refund because the singer stopped her concert after just twenty minutes.
因為歌手在開場僅僅二十分鐘後就終止演場會，一半的觀眾都紛紛要求退票。

one third **名** 三分之一 （第 5 題）

例句 • Nearly one third of the students enjoy swimming.
將近三分之一的學生喜歡游泳。

• One third of the company's annual marketing budget was spent on this campaign.
這間公司三分之一的年度行銷預算花在這項活動上。

◎ 學習策略

1. 練習描述照片的主題與內容

平常看到照片或圖片時，練習以簡單英文描述內容。如果圖中重點是「人物」，試著說出人物的動作、穿著、表情、場景、職業等。記得行為動作要用「現在進行式」，例如：He is taking notes.（他正在做筆記）。如果重點是事物，要描述場景、物品位置關係、狀態等，常用的時態是「現在簡單式」和「現在完成式」，並要留意表示位置關係的介係詞，例如：The paintings are on the wall.（畫作掛在牆上）。這個練習不僅有助於準備聽力「看圖辨義」，對於備考中級和中高級口說的「看圖敘述」也很有益處。

2. 利用生活中各種情境聯想詞彙

聽力理解與字彙量息息相關。學習詞彙最有效的方法之一就是透過日常生活、學校與公共場合的各種情境隨時自主學習，例如在逛街時，可想想商品的名稱以及在商店中會用的句子該怎麼用英文表達，像是「我可以試大一號的嗎？」（Can I try on a bigger one?）、「現在這個有特價嗎？」（Is it on sale now?）、「我決定要買它」（I'll take it.）。如果有不會的，可以整理在手機或是筆記本裡，之後再問老師或是上網查詢正確說法，並且規劃複習時程，反覆溫習這個筆記裡的單字與句子。

3. 利用圖像幫助記憶單字

很多時候，聽不懂是因為單字量不足，平日隨身準備一本圖解字典（picture dictionary），可以幫助擴充常用字詞量。另外，也可利用本大題的圖片，學習相關的詞彙，並使用簡單且完整的短句描述圖片。以第二題的圖片為例，圖片中的物品包含：窗簾（curtain）、燈（lamp）、鬧鐘（alarm clock）、拖鞋（slippers）等，並利用這些單字造句，例如：The woman is drawing/opening the curtains.（這位女生正在拉窗簾）。這樣的練習可幫助累積字彙量並預測考題。善用資源與規劃學習的能力也是重要的核心素養。

可以多留意生活中練習英文的機會，逐次累積，應考聽力測驗時能掌握更多字彙。

ANSWERING QUESTIONS

中級聽力

第二部份

問答

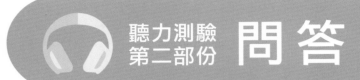
這個部份包含日常生活中常見的十個問句與直述句,聽完之後根據題目的語意選擇最適當的回應。

本部份評量的學習表現包括：

- ✓ 能理解日常生活用語與常用句型
- ✓ 能依據句子的語意與情境選擇適當的回應
- ✓ 能根據句子語調理解說話者的情緒與態度

考前提醒

這個部份評量是否能理解口語中的問句或直述句,並選擇適當的回應方式。問句與直述句的內容多與日常生活相關,與核心素養強調的符號運用與溝通表達的原則一致。平時多熟悉口語中各式句型與常用詞彙及其正確發音,練習完整地理解語意與情境,就不難找出最適當的回應。作答時,避免僅憑句中一兩個字拼湊猜測答案。

回答這類型的題目時

1. 首先掌握題目的句型（例如：Wh 問句、Yes-No 問句與直述句）

   先熟悉這些句型，有助於即時理解句意並選擇適當回應。

常見句型	學習建議	說明
Wh 問句	先聽清楚該句的 wh- 疑問詞，再選擇合適的回答。常見的 wh- 疑問詞包含 who、what、when、where、how、which、why 等。	**例句** Who does this jacket belong to? 這件夾克是誰的？ **可能的回應** A customer probably left it. 可能是顧客留下的。 **說明** 這個題目的 wh- 疑問詞為 who，詢問外套是誰的，因此回應會與「人」相關。
Yes-No 問句	Yes-No 問句的回應主要可分為直接回答與間接回答。 1. 直接回答：包含 Yes、No 或是類似用語的肯定或否定回答，例如：Sure, no problem. 2. 間接回答：可能是不確定的回應，例如：Well, I'm not sure.，或是以另一個問句來反問，例如：Will size eleven do? Yes-No 問句不一定會用 Yes/No 回答，一定要依語意與選項內容判斷。	**例句** Will you go camping with us in the mountains this weekend? 你這週末要跟我們去山上露營嗎？ **可能的回應** 直接回答 1. Yes. I'd love to. 　好啊，我想去。 2. I'm afraid I'm not available. 　我恐怕沒有空。 間接回答 1. Let me check my schedule. 　讓我確認一下我的行程表。 2. Cool. But how's the weather looking? 　太棒了，不過天氣如何呢？ **說明** 這個題目詢問週末是否有空去露營，因此可能的回應會針對「是否可以去」做回應。

直述句	直述句的回應和句子的情境、語意與溝通目的相關。先聽懂關鍵字了解該句情境與語意，再做回應。	**例句** Look, Tracy! You and Sophia are wearing exactly the same dress. Tracy，你跟 Sophia 穿了一樣的洋裝。 **可能的回應** What a coincidence! 好巧喔！ **說明** 這個題目陳述 Tracy 和 Sophia 穿了一樣的洋裝的這項事實，故回應會針對句中的重點資訊（wearing the same dress）做回應。

2. 接著仔細閱讀每個選項

　　除了聽清楚題目之外，仔細閱讀選項也很重要。正確答案會是最適當的回應，但切勿看到誘答選項有與題目相同的字就認為是答案，要仔細讀完每個選項再選出最合適的回應。

參考以上策略，可以幫助選擇正確回應唷！

Note

第 6 題

Why didn't you tell me earlier?
There's nothing I can do now.

A.　I felt relieved that you were safe.

B.　I can never thank you enough.

C.　I usually get ready beforehand.

D.　I thought you already knew.

你怎麼不早點告訴我?現在做什麼都來不及了。

A.　你安全我就放心了。

B.　真的太謝謝你了。

C.　我通常會事先準備好。

D.　我以為你早就知道了。

正解 D

本題取材自生活場景，是 Why 開始的問句，掌握句子鋪陳的情境並針對「原因」回應。

說話者想知道對方為什麼沒有告訴他某件事（why didn't you tell me earlier?），當中的 why 和 tell 是重要關鍵字，告訴我們說話者在乎的訊息是「原因」與「告知」。四選項中只有 D：I thought you already knew.（我以為你早就知道了）最符合情境，因此 D 是最適合的回應。

關鍵字詞 earlier 提早（的）、較早（的）

第 7 題

Would you care for some dessert?　　你想要來些甜點嗎？

A. Yes. Could I have the menu again?
A. 好，我可以再看一下菜單嗎？

B. Can I help you with something?
B. 我可以幫你什麼嗎？

C. Have you been here before?
C. 你來過這裡嗎？

D. No. I'm sure no one has ever done it.
D. 不，我確定沒人做過。

正解 Ⓐ

本題的情境是在餐廳，是一句 Yes-No 問句，本句是由 would 和 care 引導出的禮貌詢問方式。掌握這個常見句型，就能迅速推論情境。

根據這個句子的語意，我們可推測說話的人是餐廳的侍者。他問顧客要不要來一客甜點，顧客最適切的回應是要求看完菜單再做決定，因此本題的最適合的回應是 A：Yes. Could I have the menu again?（好，我可以再看一下菜單嗎？）

關鍵字詞 care（用於禮貌地提議或建議）想要、喜歡　dessert 甜食、甜點　menu 菜單

Did you ask your teacher for the day off tomorrow?

你跟老師請明天的假了嗎？

A. Yes, I see what you mean.

A. 是，我了解你的意思。

B. Yes, I spoke with him earlier.

B. 是，我先前跟他說了。

C. No, I must not have seen it.

C. 不，我一定沒看到。

D. No, I didn't bring it with me.

D. 不，我沒帶來。

正解 B

本題取材自校園情境，是 Did 開始的 Yes-No 問句，所以是問過去發生的事，掌握句子的時態與關鍵字詞即可選出適當回應。

本題的說話者問：Did you ask your teacher for the day off tomorrow?（你跟老師請明天的假了嗎？）。這個句子除了說話者、句子中的 you，還有第三個角色 teacher，這是個重要的答題關鍵，可以先檢查四個選項中哪個有出現這個第三人稱，這個選項就有可能是正確答案。選項 B：Yes, I spoke with him earlier.（是，我先前跟他說了。）中提到 him，情境與時態也符合題目，故 B 是最適合的回應。

關鍵字詞 ask 詢問、請求　day off 休息日　speak 談話、說

第 9 題

In which part of the city will the amusement park be built?

A. This way, please.

B. Close to the suburbs, I guess.

C. It's the biggest in the world.

D. Just a ten-minute walk.

遊樂園會建在城市的哪個區域？

A. 這邊請。

B. 我猜會靠近郊區。

C. 它是世界上最大的。

D. 只要走路十分鐘。

正解 (B)

本題情境為一般社交生活，是 In which 開始的疑問句，需聽清楚開頭的疑問詞並理解動詞 be built 和名詞 amusement park 等關鍵字詞。

本題說話者問：In which part of the city will the amusement park be built?（遊樂園會建在城市的哪個區域？），此句的 in which 即為 where，因此適切的回答應與「地點」有關。選項 B 表示應該會靠近郊區，故為最合適的回應。選項 A 回答方向，選項 C 的重點是大小，選項 D 則強調距離，皆與題目內容無關，因此都不是答案。

關鍵字詞 suburb 城郊、郊區

Jack showed me his coin collection the other day. It was amazing.

A. No wonder. He's very lucky.

B. Indeed. He's spent a lot of time on it.

C. Not at all. You're so kind.

D. Count me in. I'd love to come along.

Jack 前幾天給我看他收藏的硬幣，很令人驚嘆。

A. 難怪，他很幸運。

B. 的確，他花很多時間在上面。

C. 不客氣，你人真好。

D. 算我一份，我想一起去。

正解 Ⓑ

本題取材自生活場景，為直述句，重點資訊為 coin collection（硬幣收藏）和 amazing（令人驚嘆）這兩個詞彙。

本題說話者對於 Jack 的硬幣收藏表示驚嘆之意，因此回應也會與此相關。選項 B 對於說話者的意見表示認同，並補充額外資訊 Jack 花了很多時間在收集，情境與語意皆適當，故為最適合的回應。選項 A 與 D 的情境不符，選項 C 是用於致謝的禮貌回應，因此都不是答案。

關鍵字詞 collection 收藏　amazing 驚人的、令人驚喜的

第 11 題

It was a wonderful party, Sue, but we really must be going.

A. So soon? It's only 10:00.

B. Yes, I think she enjoyed it.

C. I'm so happy you'll be able to come.

D. That's too bad. I'm busy that evening.

Sue，這是個很棒的派對，但我們真的必須要離開了。

A. 這麼快？才 10 點耶。

B. 是的，我覺得她喜歡。

C. 我很開心你們能來。

D. 太不巧了，那個傍晚我有事。

正解

本題取材自生活中的社交用語，是一句直述句，可以針對關鍵資訊（we really must be going）回應。

從前半句可以得知說話者正在參加 Sue 舉辦的派對，但是說話者隨即表示 we really must be going（我們真的必須要離開了）。回應說話者必須要離開的這個資訊，選項中只有 A 符合情境（這麼快？才 10 點耶）。

句中的 Sue 是正在與說話者對談的人，如果沒有掌握這個關鍵，就可能誤選 B。選項 C 雖然是社交場合常見的問候語，但是沒有回應說話者要離開的資訊，選項 D 的情境與題目不符，因此都不是最適當的答案。

關鍵字詞 must 必須　soon 很快

Nicole is still angry with George for what he said the other day.

A. He must've offended her.

B. You're not in charge, are you?

C. I missed his call.

D. Did she look convinced?

Nicole 還在因為 George 前幾天說的話生氣。

A. 他一定惹惱了她。

B. 不是你負責吧，是嗎？

C. 我漏接他的電話。

D. 她看起來相信嗎？

正解 Ⓐ

本題取材自生活場景，為直述句，需針對關鍵字詞 angry with（生氣某人）和 what he said（他說的話）回應。

本題說話者表示 Nicole 還在為了 George 前幾天說的話生氣，選項 A 對這個訊息作出合理的推測，認為 George 一定惹惱了 Nicole，回應符合情境，因此為最適合的回應。其他選項與題目的情境皆不合。

關鍵字詞 offend 冒犯、得罪、惹惱

第 13 題

Susan, how was the concert last night? I heard it was delayed.

A. Yes. My train was 15 minutes late.

B. Maybe not. There was a long line.

C. OK. I bought four front seats.

D. No. Everything was perfect.

Susan，昨天的演唱會如何？我聽說表演延遲開場。

A. 對啊，我的火車延誤 15 分鐘。

B. 或許沒有，隊伍排得很長。

C. 好的，我買了四張前排座位的票。

D. 沒有，一切都很完美。

正解 Ⓓ

本題取材自一般社交情境，是 how 開始的疑問句，需掌握疑問詞 how 的合適回應，以及透過關鍵字 concert 和 delay 聯想對話情境。

說話者問昨晚的演唱會（concert）如何，並提到聽說演唱會延遲開場（delayed）。回應時，應針對此情境和資訊直接回答。選項 D 先以 No 反駁演唱會延誤開場的傳聞，後補充 Everything was perfect.（一切都很完美）來回答昨晚演唱會的狀況。問題句中沒有選項 A 所提的 train（火車）。選項 B 的 maybe not 常用於委婉表示否定或拒絕，雖然回應了沒有延誤，但是後面的「隊伍排得很長」又與沒有延誤的情境相牴觸。選項 C 的重點則在於所購買的座位位置，因此都不是正確答案。

關鍵字詞 concert 演唱會　delay（使）延遲、（使）延誤、（使）延期

Have you been to the gym at the new community sports center yet?

A. Yes. I'll go to the open house.

B. Yes. Their equipment is first class.

C. Yes. That pair fits him very well.

D. Yes. You have to take a shower first.

你去過新社區運動中心裡的健身房了嗎?

A. 對,開放日那天我會去。

B. 對,那裡的設備都是一流的。

C. 對,那雙很適合他。

D. 對,你需要先洗澡。

正解 B

本題取材自生活情境,是以 Have 開始的 Yes-No 問句,此句是現在完成式,是在詢問經驗。

句子中的關鍵字為 gym(健身房),如果回應有出現和健身房相關的資訊,就很有可能是正確答案。選項 B 的 equipment(設備)指的就是健身器材,回答者不僅已經去了新社區運動中心裡的健身房,還認為當中的健身設備相當棒。

選項 A 的 open house 通常是指平常不開放的場所在特別的時間開放讓大眾參觀,並不適合指健身房。選項 C 中的 that pair 在題目句中找不到可對應的字詞,選項 D 則是在解釋順序,都不是正確答案。

關鍵字詞 gym 健身房、體育館 equipment 設備、器材

第 15 題

If I had known it would be such a sunny day, I would've brought my suntan lotion.

A. Can I put it on?

B. I'll take a chance.

C. You can use mine.

D. Will you sponsor me?

早知道會是大晴天，我就會帶我的助曬乳。

A. 我可以塗上去嗎？

B. 我會試試看。

C. 你可以用我的。

D. 你會贊助我嗎？

正解　C

本題取材自生活情境，是一句以 If 開始的直述句，掌握本句的假設句法可以幫助理解情境。

本句的句構 If + 過去完成式，表示與過去事實相反，說話者不知道今天會是晴天，所以沒有帶助曬乳。選項 C：You can use mine.（你可以用我的）正是回應「說話者沒有帶助曬乳」的訊息，因此為最適合的回應。說話者沒有帶助曬乳，故選項 A 不合理，選項 B 與 D 則與情境不符。

關鍵字詞 sunny 晴朗　suntan lotion 助曬乳

接著我們來複習本部份的重點詞彙

earlier 形 提早（的）、較早（的）（第 6 題）

例句
- Why didn't you tell me earlier?
  你怎麼不早點告訴我？

- Passengers taking international flights will have to arrive at the airport earlier than those who take domestic flights.
  搭乘國際航線的旅客需要比搭乘國內航線的旅客早抵達機場。

care 動 （用於禮貌地提議或建議）想要、喜歡（第 7 題）

例句
- Would you care for some dessert?
  你想要來些甜點嗎？

- I don't particularly care for action movies.
  我不是特別喜歡動作電影。

dessert 名 甜食、甜點（第 7 題）

例句
- The dessert shop next to the train station has the most delicious chocolate cake in town.
  火車站旁那間甜點店賣的巧克力蛋糕是全鎮最好吃的。

menu 名 菜單（第 7 題）

例句
- Could I have the menu again?
  我可以再看一下菜單嗎？

- Are there any vegetarian dishes on the menu? I don't eat meat or seafood.
  菜單上有任何素食餐點嗎？我不吃肉或海鮮。

ask 動 詢問、請求 （第 8 題）

例句 • Did you ask your teacher for the day off tomorrow?
你跟老師請明天的假了嗎？

• Asked about the details of the wedding, the bride-to-be answered with a bright smile on her face.
當被問到婚禮的細節時，新娘臉上洋溢燦爛的微笑。

day off 休息日 （第 8 題）

例句 • Jacob is planning on taking a day off next week.
Jacob 正在計畫下周休假一天。

speak 動 談話、說 （第 8 題）

例句 • I spoke with him earlier.
我先前跟他說了。

• In this tunnel, we'll have to speak very softly so that we won't disturb the bats.
在這個隧道裡面，我們要儘量壓低我們的音量才不會打擾到蝙蝠。

延伸學習　speak of the devil 說到曹操，曹操就到

suburb 名 城郊、郊區 （第 9 題）

例句 • The amusement park will be built close to the suburbs.
遊樂園會建在靠近郊區的地方。

• Many people are now more willing to live in the suburbs, such as Linkou or Guishan, where the cost of living is lower than in Taipei.
很多人現在都比較喜歡住在像林口或是龜山這樣的郊區，因為那裡的生活開銷比台北來得低。

collection 名 收藏 （第 10 題）

例句 • Jack showed me his coin collection the other day. It was amazing.
Jack 前幾天給我看他收藏的硬幣，很令人驚嘆。

• My grandmother has an extensive collection of stamps from Japanese post office.
我奶奶有一套很完整的日本郵票的收藏。

amazing 形 驚人的、令人驚喜的 （第 10 題）

例句 • The child wrote in his diary that he saw an amazing butterfly with huge colorful wings on a rose blossom.
小朋友在他的日記裡寫道他在一朵玫瑰花上看到一隻有著又大又鮮艷的翅膀、令人驚豔的蝴蝶。

must 助 必須 （第 11 題）

例句 • It was a wonderful party, Sue, but we really must be going.
Sue，這是個很棒的派對，但我們真的必須要離開了。

• You must finish the required courses before you can take any advanced courses.
你必須要先修完必修課才能修進階課程。

soon 副 很快 （第 11 題）

例句 • The play will start soon! Hurry up or we'll miss the opening scene.
舞台劇快開始了！快點，不然我們要錯過第一幕了。

offend 動 冒犯、得罪、惹惱 （第 12 題）

例句 • He must've offended her.
他一定惹惱了她。

• Louis didn't mean to offend Lisa by making fun of her new hairstyle.
Louis 並不是故意要惹惱 Lisa 才開她新髮型的玩笑。

concert 名 演唱會 （第 13 題）

例句 • Susan, how was the concert last night?
Susan，昨天的演唱會如何？

• Many of my friends posted on social media that they had successfully bought tickets to the singer's concert.
我很多朋友都在社群網頁上分享他們成功搶到那位歌手的演唱會門票。

delay **動** （使）延遲、（使）延誤、（使）延期（第 13 題）

例句 • I heard the show was delayed.
我聽說表演延遲開場。

• Luckily, the ferry we are going to take will not be delayed by the typhoon.
幸好我們要搭的那班渡輪並沒有因為颱風延遲。

gym **名** 健身房、體育館（第 14 題）

例句 • Have you been to the gym at the new community sports center yet?
你去過新社區運動中心裡的健身房了嗎？

• Eric felt quite delightful that he got a 50% discount on the gym membership.
Eric 得到五折的健身房會員優惠，覺得特別開心。

equipment **名** 設備、器材（第 14 題）

例句 • The equipment at the gym is first class.
這個健身房的設備都是一流的。

• The hospital introduces their state-of-the-art medical equipment on their website.
這家醫院在網站上介紹了他們先進的醫療設備。

sunny **形** 晴朗（第 15 題）

例句 • If I had known it would be such a sunny day, I would've brought my suntan lotion.
早知道會是大晴天，我就會帶我的助曬乳。

• My cats like to lie on the porch and take a sunbath on sunny days.
我的貓喜歡在晴天時躺在門廊曬太陽。

suntan lotion 助曬乳（第 15 題）

例句 • Remember to grab a bottle of suntan lotion at the drugstore for our tip to Kenting.
記得去藥妝店買罐助曬乳，我們去墾丁玩要用。

1. 掌握正確發音

有些學習者指出同樣的英文內容，用讀的可以理解意思，但是聲音播出來卻不一定能聽懂，可能的原因是沒有掌握正確發音。例如：母音唸錯，將 frequent [`frikwənt] 唸錯為 *[frɛ`kwent]、或將 leather[`lɛðɚ] 唸錯為 *[`liðɚ]。平時學習詞彙時，除了字義、用法及拼字外，也可利用網路字典聆聽該詞彙的發音並開口唸，確切掌握正確發音。

2. 熟悉口語中常用的片語及慣用語

聆聽題目時，有時候似乎每個字都聽清楚了，卻仍然不懂整句的意思，這可能是碰到了不熟悉的片語或慣用語，例如：count on somebody（依靠某人）、Way to go!（做得好！）。學習新單字時，留意與這個單字相關的片語與慣用語，漸漸就能熟悉這些固定的用法，對自己的聽力及會話能力均有助益。

3. 練習各種場合中常用的句型及應答方式

平日積極參與課內及課外英語文團體學習活動，與老師或同學用英語對話，練習口語中各類常見的應答方式，才能迅速理解句子的語意。若平日較難找到機會與他人對話，亦可利用本書的題目練習，可聆聽所附的音檔並自行練習有可能的回應。以第 7 題為例，當聽到：Would you care for some dessert? 除了正確答案：Yes. Could I have the menu again? 可自行延伸練習不同回應，例如直接回答：Yes. I would like to have chocolate cake. 或是有禮貌地拒絕 Thanks. I'm full. 亦或是間接回答，例如：What would you recommend?

把握生活中使用英語的機會，仔細聆聽英文母語者的對話、複誦練習，不僅可以提升英語聽力，也可以加強口說的能力。

Note

CONVERSATIONS

中級聽力
第三部份

簡短對話

聽力測驗 第三部份　簡短對話

這個部份每題包含一段對話及一個相關的問題，聽完對話後，根據對話與題目的內容選擇最適當的答案。

> **本部份評量的學習表現包括：**
>
> ✓　能聽懂英語日常對話，並
>   - ★　能根據上下文釐清訊息
>   - ★　能分析、歸納多項訊息
>   - ★　能綜合相關資訊預測可能的發展或做合理猜測
>   - ★　能理解說話者的觀點、態度與言外之意

考前提醒

這個部份主要評量能否跨越單句的層次，理解上下文，以掌握對話中重要訊息。對話種類包含家庭會話、社交談話、工作或課堂討論、電話交談等。這部份也包含圖表題，反映日常生活中常需要一邊聆聽、一邊參考書面資料的真實情境和理解過程，需整合歸納聽到與看到的訊息作答。

考試時，可運用以下幾個策略幫助理解、分析、統整與詮釋對話內容

1. 整合對話中的關鍵資訊

答題的相關資訊有時會分散出現於對話中（例如第 22 題），儘量避免只根據一兩句話就直接作答，應仔細聽完對話與題目，整合對話中的關鍵資訊，推知正確答案。

2. 分析訊息之間的關聯性，釐清上下文關係

理解對話中訊息之間的關係，才能正確掌握對話的內容。這些訊息可能以幾種較常見的方式出現，例如：詢問與回答、提議與回覆等等。分析訊息之間的關聯性，就能迅速深入理解對話的內容（例如第 20 題）。

3. 推論說話者的言外之意或觀點

聽到對話的內容時，除了理解字面意義外，也需運用自己的知識與生活經驗，建構出更完整的語意，並推論說話者的言外之意與觀點，或是預測可能的發展。例如：He's not the only plumber around, you know.（水電工又不是只有他一個。），雖然說話者未明確表示自己的意見，卻暗示應該另請高明。

4. 解讀圖表資訊，預測題目，再與對話內容整合

需要聽讀整合的圖表題（例如第 24、25 題）雖然看似複雜，其實是真實生活常遇到的情況，只要答題時依照下面幾個步驟，就能輕鬆掌握對話內容，推知正確答案。
(1) 先看清楚圖表與選項提供的資訊
(2) 預測對話的內容與可能的題目
(3) 聆聽對話時，對照圖中的資訊，找出關鍵線索，就能順利找出答案。

掌握這些技巧，多練習之後，英語聽解能力一定會有明顯的進步！

(M)	Who's that on the cover of your magazine?
(W)	Richard Howard. He's starred in several movies lately. Have you seen any of them?
(M)	No, but I've heard good things about him.
(W)	Actually, quite a few people think he's handsome but has little talent.
(M)	Oh? I'm surprised to hear that.

（男）	妳雜誌封面上的人物是誰？
（女）	Richard Howard。他最近演了好幾部電影，你有看嗎？
（男）	沒有，但我聽到不少好評。
（女）	其實有不少人認為他雖然很帥，但沒有演戲天分。
（男）	是嗎？我很意外有人那樣想。

What is the main subject of this conversation?

A. A successful chain of theaters.
B. A trend in the entertainment industry.
C. The director of a classic film.
D. General opinion about an actor.

這段對話的主題是什麼？

A. 一家成功的連鎖電影院
B. 演藝圈的一股潮流
C. 一部經典電影的導演
D. 大眾對於一位演員的看法

 正解 Ⓓ

本題的內容取材自日常對話，需整合對話中的關鍵線索，判斷主題。

這段對話一開始，男生便問 Who's that on the cover of your magazine?（誰是雜誌封面人物？）女生回答是 Richard Howard. 搭配關鍵句 He's starred in several movies lately.（他最近演了多部電影）便可判斷兩人談論的主題是位演員，而非導演，再加上女生轉述別人的評論 He's handsome but has little talent.（他很帥但沒天分），就知道本題正確答案為 D。

關鍵字詞 opinion 意見、看法　actor 演員

第 17 題

(W)　Hello? Accounting Division.

(M)　Hello, Diane. It's Jack. I have a question for you.

(W)　Certainly. What's up?

(M)　I was looking at the proposal you gave me yesterday, and.... Oh, I'm sorry, Diane, someone just came into my office and I need to talk to her. Can I call you back?

(W)　Sure. I'll be here at my desk.

(M)　I'll call you back in a few minutes.

Why will the man call the woman back?

A.　He can't find the file he needs.

B.　He'll be away from his office.

C.　He was interrupted by someone.

D.　He has to reply to an email first.

（女）　會計科，您好。

（男）　哈囉，Diane，我是 Jack。我有個問題想請教妳。

（女）　好。怎麼了？

（男）　我在看妳昨天給我的提案，然後…不好意思，Diane，有人來辦公室找我，我需要跟她談一下。我可以晚點再打給妳嗎？

（女）　當然，我會在我的位置上。

（男）　我過幾分鐘後回撥給妳。

為什麼男子要回電給女子？

A.　他找不到他要的檔案。

B.　他將離開辦公室。

C.　他被某人打斷。

D.　他必須先回覆一封電子郵件。

正解 Ⓒ

本題內容取材自工作場所的電話交談。作答時需聽懂關鍵句，結合自身平日電話交談的經驗，便可得知為何 Jack 要回電給 Diane。

Jack 話說到一半時對 Diane 說：I'm sorry, Diane, someone just came into my office.... Can I call you back?（Diane，不好意思，有人來辦公室找我…，我可以晚點再打給妳嗎？）由此可得知兩人在電話交談的過程中，有人進入 Jack 的辦公室找他，對話因此必須中斷，所以正確答案為 C。

關鍵字詞 call back 回電　interrupt 打斷（談話）

(M)	Have you been busy recently?
(W)	Too busy. With my new job, plus taking care of my kids and running errands, I feel like I'm always on the go. I'm exhausted.
(M)	I know what you mean. Sometimes I wish the world would just slow down.
(W)	I doubt that will ever happen.

（男）	妳最近忙嗎？
（女）	忙翻了。新工作加上照顧小孩和處理其他雜事，我覺得總是忙個不停，超累的。
（男）	我懂妳的意思。有時候我希望生活的步調能慢一點。
（女）	我不覺得會有這一天。

What are these people mainly discussing?

A. Their family members.
B. The fast pace of their lives.
C. Their next destination.
D. The terrible traffic.

說話者主要在討論什麼？

A. 他們的家庭成員
B. 緊湊的生活步調
C. 他們下個目的地
D. 糟糕的交通

正解 **B**

本題內容取材自朋友間的日常問候，作答時只須聽懂少數關鍵句，根據句子的字面意義理解言談，便可得知兩人對話的主題。

這段對話一開始，男生問 Have you been busy lately?（妳最近忙嗎？），女生直接回說 Too busy.（忙翻了），然後簡短交代了一下她忙碌的原因，男生回說：Sometimes I wish the world would just slow down.（有時候我希望生活的步調能慢一點。），從以上這幾句對話便可得知本題正確答案為 B：The fast pace of their lives.（緊湊的生活步調）。

關鍵字詞 on the go 忙個不停 exhausted 筋疲力竭的 pace 步調、節奏

第 19 題

(W)	Everyone in our class seems to enjoy telling jokes.	（女）	我們班上每個人似乎都喜歡講笑話。
(M)	Yes, but I seldom find them to be very funny.	（男）	是啊，但我大多覺得不好笑。
(W)	I noticed that you don't laugh very much. Why are you so serious, Bill?	（女）	我注意到你不怎麼愛笑。Bill，你為什麼這麼嚴肅？
(M)	I don't know. I guess it's just my personality.	（男）	我也不知道，大概我的個性就是這樣吧。

What does the man seem to lack?

這男生可能缺少什麼？

A.	A sense of humor.	A.	幽默感
B.	A desire to succeed.	B.	對成功的渴望
C.	An appreciation of art.	C.	藝術鑑賞力
D.	An instinct for survival.	D.	生存本能

 正解 Ⓐ

本題內容取材自同學間的日常對話，需綜合對話中的關鍵線索，推敲男生可能缺少什麼。

女生一開始先說班上很多人都喜歡講笑話，但男生認為大多都不好笑。女生便問他 Why are you so serious?（你為何這麼嚴肅？），男生回答：I guess it's just my personality.（大概我的個性就是這樣吧。），綜合以上線索可得知這男生可能沒有什麼幽默感，因此本題正確答案為 A。

關鍵字詞 personality 個性　lack 缺乏　humor 幽默

(M)	Metropolitan Museum. How may I help you?
(W)	Yes, I'm writing a short article about the Japanese art exhibition you're having next month. Can you tell me when it will start?
(M)	July 3, and it runs for six weeks.
(W)	I heard one of the artists is visiting Taiwan.
(M)	Yes, and he'll attend the opening ceremony at 10 A.M. on the third.
(W)	Good, that's all I need to know.
(M)	Where will the article appear?
(W)	In the *Daily Post*.

（男）	大都會博物館，您好，有什麼能為您服務的？
（女）	是這樣的，我正在寫一篇有關你們下個月日本藝術展的報導。可以麻煩你告訴我展覽什麼時候開始嗎？
（男）	7 月 3 號開始，為期六週。
（女）	我聽說其中一位藝術家會來臺灣。
（男）	對，他會出席 3 號早上 10 點的開幕典禮。
（女）	好，這就是我需要的資訊。
（男）	請問這篇報導會刊登在哪裡？
（女）	《每日郵報》。

What does the woman do for a living?

A. She's a photographer.
B. She's a businesswoman.
C. She's a reporter.
D. She's a teacher.

女子是做什麼工作的？

A. 她是位攝影師。
B. 她是位商人。
C. 她是位記者。
D. 她是位老師。

 正解 Ⓒ

本題內容取材自簡短的電話訪談，需釐清上下文關係，並根據語境推敲含意，此段對話主要是以一問一答的方式進行，可根據女子的問題與回覆男子的內容來推敲女子的身分。

對話一開始女子便表明自己正在為日本藝術展寫一篇報導，接著詢問對方展覽相關的資訊，例如：展期、參展藝術家是否來臺等，最後說報導會刊登在《每日郵報》。綜合以上線索即可推斷女子的職業是記者。

關鍵字詞 article 報導、文章 exhibition 展覽 reporter 記者

第 21 題

(W) Paul? One of the pipes under the kitchen sink is leaking.

(M) Again? I just fixed that a week ago.

(W) I know.

(M) I guess I'd better call Randy Robinson this time. He can do a better job of fixing it than I can.

(W) Does he do this kind of work for a living now?

(M) Yes, and his charges are reasonable.

What is the man planning to do this time?

A. File a complaint about a plumber.

B. Hire an experienced plumber.

C. Borrow some plumbing tools.

D. Learn more plumbing skills.

（女） Paul ？廚房水槽下面有一條管線在漏水。

（男） 又漏水？我上禮拜才修過耶。

（女） 我知道。

（男） 我想我這次最好打電話給 Randy Robinson。他修理的技術比我好。

（女） 他現在以此為業嗎？

（男） 對啊，而且他收費合理。

男子這次打算怎麼做？

A. 對水電工提出客訴

B. 雇用經驗豐富的水電工

C. 借一些維修管線的工具

D. 學更多維修管線的技能

正解 B

本題內容取材自家庭日常對話，需整合對話中的線索，判斷男子下一步的動作。

對話一開始女子先說廚房漏水了，男子回答：Again? I just fixed that a week ago.（又漏水？我上禮拜才修過），從這句話可推測男子修水管的技術似乎有待加強，接著男子建議尋求專業協助，最後還補充說 Randy Robinson 收費合理。統整上述各項線索，即可判斷男子打算雇用有經驗的水電工。

關鍵字詞 leak 漏水　do (...) for a living 以…為業　hire 雇用　plumber 水電工、水管工人

(M) What are those strips of paper you're putting on your door?

(男) 妳貼在門上長條狀的紙是什麼？

(W) These are for good luck.

(女) 這是為了祈求好運。

(M) I've never seen anything like that before.

(男) 我之前沒看過這種東西。

(W) We put up new ones at Chinese New Year and leave them on the door all year.

(女) 我們過農曆新年的時候會在門上黏新的紙條，貼一整年。

(M) Does everyone in your country do that?

(男) 你們國家每個人都會這樣做嗎？

(W) Not everyone does, but a lot of people do. It's a tradition.

(女) 沒有每個人，但很多人都這樣做，這是傳統。

What are the speakers talking about?

說話者在討論什麼？

A. A traditional dish.

A. 一道傳統菜餚

B. A holiday custom.

B. 一個節慶習俗

C. A planned trip to China.

C. 一個去中國的旅行計畫

D. New numbers for his door.

D. 他的新門牌號碼

正解 B

本題內容取材自與外國友人的日常對話，答題線索分布於整篇對話，需歸納整合對話中的關鍵訊息，才能判斷主題。

這段對話幾乎都是男生發問，女生回答。根據男生的問題：What are those strips of paper you're putting on your door?（妳貼在門上長條狀的紙是什麼？）以及女生的回答：These are for good luck.（為了祈求好運）和 We put up new ones at Chinese New Year.（過農曆新年時會貼）等言談可以得知兩件事：一、這男生從來沒有看過春聯，是位外國人；二、他們談論的主題是農曆新年相關的習俗。整合以上訊息便可判斷本題正確答案為 B：A holiday custom（節慶習俗）。

關 鍵 字 詞 strip 長條 tradition 傳統 custom 習俗

第 23 題

(W)	What are you looking for?		（女）	你在找什麼？
(M)	The manual for this coffee machine. I can't remember how to use it.		（男）	這台咖啡機的使用手冊。我忘記怎麼用了。
(W)	Is the manual small?		（女）	手冊是小本的嗎？
(M)	Yes.		（男）	對。
(W)	Then check the cabinet in the study. I recently put some small manuals there.		（女）	那你看一下書房的櫃子，我最近放了一些小手冊在那邊。

What is the man looking for?

A. A booklet.
B. A receipt.
C. A bill.
D. A ticket.

男子在找什麼？

A. 一本小冊子
B. 一張收據
C. 一張帳單
D. 一張票

正解 Ⓐ

本題內容取材自居家生活對話，需根據句子的字面意義理解言談。作答時如有掌握對話中一兩個關鍵字詞，便可得知男子在尋找什麼東西。

在女子詢問 What are you looking for?（你在找什麼）後，男子立刻表明自己在找咖啡機的使用手冊，因此如可以掌握 manual 這個關鍵字，即可得知正確答案為 A：A booklet.（一本小冊子）。

關鍵字詞 manual 使用手冊　booklet 小冊子

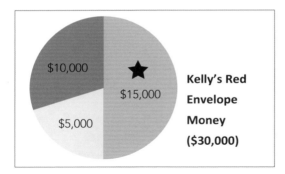

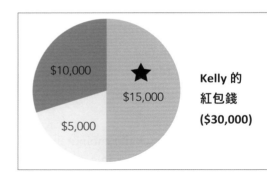

For question number 24, please look at the pie chart.

關於第 24 題，請看圓餅圖。

(M)　Kelly, what are you going to do with your red envelope this year?

(W)　I'm going to spend all of it on a cellphone and some clothes.

(M)　I think you should put half of the money in the bank and donate one-third like what we did last year.
And then you can spend the rest on shopping.

(W)　That'll leave me...only five thousand dollars!

(M)　That should be enough.

(W)　All right, Dad.

（男）　Kelly，妳今年打算怎麼運用妳的紅包錢？

（女）　我要把全部的錢拿去買手機和衣服。

（男）　我認為妳應該把一半的錢存進銀行，並且像我們去年一樣，把三分之一捐出去，剩下的你再拿去購物。

（女）　那樣我只剩下…5,000 元耶！

（男）　那應該夠了吧。

（女）　好吧，爸爸。

Look at the pie chart. What does the area marked with a star refer to?

A.　Buying a cellphone.

B.　Getting new clothes.

C.　Donating to charity.

D.　Saving in the bank.

請看圓餅圖。有星星標記的區域將作什麼用途？

A.　買手機

B.　買新衣服

C.　捐贈給慈善機構

D.　存入銀行

正解 Ⓓ

本題內容取材自父女間的日常對話，需整合歸納聽到的內容與圖表的資訊，才能推論正確答案。我們可運用「考前提醒」第四點提到的圖表題聽解方式，幫助理解此題的對話。

1. 先瀏覽圖表與選項提供的資訊。由圓餅圖可知 Kelly 的紅包錢總共是 $30,000，分成三份，其中一份有星星標記。由選項可知紅包錢有四種可能的用途。

2. 預測對話的內容與可能的題目。根據圓餅圖與選項可預測對話內容應該與「如何運用紅包錢」有關，而題目可能會問「有星星標記的那一份作何用途」。

3. 聽到問題後，對照圖中的資訊，找出答案。本題問圓餅圖上有星星標記的金額（$15,000）是預計作什麼用途，聆聽對話時，需特別注意與紅包錢用途相關的資訊。首先，女兒想將紅包錢全部用來買衣服與手機，但是爸爸建議一半（$15,000）存銀行、捐三分之一（$10,000）給慈善機構、剩下的（$5,000）可以花掉。整合以上所有的資訊可得知正確答案為 D：Saving in the bank.（存入銀行）。

關鍵字詞 red envelop 紅包　donate 捐獻

NOTES
▪ **Grand Hotel:** Gym and pool
▪ **Express Inn:** Shuttle to and from airport
▪ **Days Hotel:** 5-min walk to attractions
▪ **Soho B&B:** Low room rates

NOTES
▪ **Grand Hotel:** 健身房和游泳池
▪ **Express Inn:** 機場接駁車
▪ **Days Hotel:** 離景點5分鐘路程
▪ **Soho B&B:** 房價低廉

For question number 25, please look at the note.

(W) Have you decided where we will stay in London?

(M) I've found a few nice hotels. Do we need to stay on a tight budget this trip?

(W) I think we can afford a little luxury. Are any of them convenient for getting to castles and art galleries in the downtown area?

(M) Hmm, neither the Express Inn nor the Grand Hotel is close to the city center.

(W) That's not ideal. Most places we want to visit are in the city center.

(M) I see. Now I know where we should stay.

Look at the note. Which hotel will the speakers most likely choose?

A. Grand Hotel.
B. Express Inn.
C. Days Hotel.
D. Soho B&B.

關於第 25 題，請看便條。

（女） 你決定好我們在倫敦要住哪裡了嗎？

（男） 我找到一些不錯的旅館。我們這趟旅行的預算很緊嗎？

（女） 我們應該可以負擔豪華一點的旅館。哪間旅館去市中心的城堡和畫廊比較方便？

（男） 嗯，Express Inn 和 Grand Hotel 都不靠近市中心。

（女） 這樣不好。我們大部份想去的地方都在市中心。

（男） 好，那我知道我們應該住哪裡了。

請看便條。這兩人可能會選哪間旅館？

A. Grand Hotel.
B. Express Inn.
C. Days Hotel.
D. Soho B&B.

正解 Ⓒ

本題內容取材自日常對話，說話者正在討論旅館，聆聽對話時，需整合聽到的內容與便條的資訊，才能得知說話者最後選擇的旅館。

對話一開始男子跟女子確認兩人旅行的預算，女子回答：We can afford a little luxury（我們可以負擔豪華點的旅館），由此可以先刪去便條上房價低廉的 Soho B&B。女子接著又表示要住離市區景點近一點，因此離市中心較遠的 Express Inn 和 Grand Hotel 也都非理想的選擇。藉由兩人的問答搭配便條的內容，可以推論出走五分鐘就可到景點的 Days Hotel 是最符合兩人需求的旅館，所以本題答案為 C。

關鍵字詞 attraction 景點　budget 預算　luxury 豪華　neither...nor 兩者都不

接著我們來複習本部份的重點詞彙

opinion 名 意見、看法 （第 16 題）

例句 • Taking my roommates' opinions into account, I bought the sofa even though I thought it was too expensive.
我接受了室友們的建議買了那組沙發，雖然我覺得它太貴。

actor 名 演員 （第 16 題）

例句 • For Anderson, the most difficult thing about being an actor is that he can barely have any privacy.
對 Anderson 而言，身為演員最困難的事情莫過於他幾乎沒有隱私。

call back 回電 （第 17 題）

例句 • I'll call you back in a few minutes.
我過幾分鐘後回撥給妳。

• Linda, call Ms. Flanders back when you have time. She was looking for you.
Linda，有空的話回電給 Flanders 小姐。她在找你。

interrupt 動 打斷（談話）（第 17 題）

例句 • His phone call was interrupted by someone.
他的電話被某人打斷。

• Sorry to interrupt your conversation, but I have to ask you not to talk in the library.
抱歉打斷你們的談話，但請你們在圖書館裡不要說話。

on the go 忙個不停 （第 18 題）

例句
- With my new job, plus taking care of my kids and running errands, I feel like I'm always on the go.
  新工作加上照顧小孩和處理其他雜事，我覺得總是忙個不停。

- My mom has been on the go since this morning, preparing for my sister's birthday party.
  我媽媽從早就一直忙個不停地在幫我妹妹準備生日派對。

exhausted 形 筋疲力竭的 （第 18 題）

例句
- I am exhausted.
  我累壞了。

- After the field trip, the little boy was so exhausted that he fell asleep as soon as he went into bed.
  戶外教學回來後，那位小男孩累得筋疲力竭，一上床就睡著了。

pace 名 步調、節奏 （第 18 題）

例句
- I fell behind in the race because I couldn't keep up with the other runners' pace.
  我因為追不上其他選手的步伐，所以在比賽中落後了。

personality 名 個性 （第 19 題）

例句
- I guess it's just my personality.
  大概我的個性就是這樣吧。

- Having a very outgoing personality, Mossa is always the one to break the ice in a party.
  Mossa 因為個性外向，她總是派對裡炒熱氣氛的人。

lack 動 缺乏 （第 19 題）

例句
- Lacking vitamin A, I can't see well at night.
  因為缺乏維生素 A 的關係，所以我晚上看不太清楚。

humor 名 幽默 （第 19 題）

例句 • Ted is quite a popular teacher because he has a good sense of humor, and he can always make his students laugh.
Ted 是一位很受歡迎的老師，因為他非常幽默，所以總能把班上的學生逗得哈哈大笑。

延伸學習 a sense of humor 幽默感

article 名 報導、文章 （第 20 題）

例句 • I'm writing a short article about the Japanese art exhibition you're having next month.
我正在寫一篇有關你們下個月日本藝術展的報導。

• This article teaches people how to increase their strength by working out regularly and effectively.
這篇文章教人如何規律且有效地藉由健身增加肌力。

exhibition 名 展覽 （第 20 題）

例句 • I can't wait to go to the travel exhibition this weekend.
我等不及週末要去參加旅展了。

reporter 名 記者 （第 20 題）

例句 • Being a travel reporter, John gets to visit many interesting places.
身為一位旅遊記者，John 可以去很多有趣的地方。

leak 動 漏水 （第 21 題）

例句 • One of the pipes under the kitchen sink is leaking.
廚房水槽下面有一條管線在漏水。

• The boat is coated in a special material to prevent it from leaking.
這艘船漆上了一層防漏的特殊塗料。

do (...) for a living 以…為業 （第 21 題）

例句
- Does he do this kind of work for a living now?
  他現在以此為業嗎？

- Mr. Miller doesn't enjoy being a lawyer. He just does it for a living.
  Miller 先生並沒有很喜歡當律師。對他來說那只是一份工作。

hire 動 雇用 （第 21 題）

例句
- This company hires many ex-prisoners and gives them a second chance to live an honest life.
  這家公司雇用了許多更生人，提供他們一個重新做人的機會。

plumber 名 水電工、水管工人 （第 21 題）

例句
- Do you think we should call a plumber to fix our faucet?
  你覺得我們是否應該請水電工來修這個水龍頭？

strip 名 長條 （第 22 題）

例句
- What are those strips of paper you're putting on your door?
  你貼在門上長條狀的紙是什麼？

- After reading the letter from Mary, John angrily tore it into strips and put them in the trash.
  在讀完 Mary 的信之後，John 氣得把信撕掉後丟進垃圾桶。

tradition 名 傳統 （第 22 題）

例句
- It's a tradition.
  這是傳統。

- The tradition in this tribe is to hold a festival in summer, where people dance and sing together.
  這個部落的傳統是在夏天時舉辦一個慶典，人們會一起唱歌跳舞。

custom 名 習俗 （第 22 題）

例句
- It's a custom for people to visit a temple when they are seeking advice.
  習俗上，當人民需要尋求意見時會到廟裡參拜。

manual 名 使用手冊 （第 23 題）

例句
- I'm looking for the manual for this coffee machine.
  我正在找這台咖啡機的使用手冊。

- Let's check the manual; I don't know how to operate this dryer.
  看一下使用手冊吧！我不知道怎麼操作這台烘衣機。

booklet 名 小冊子 （第 23 題）

例句
- Visitors to National Palace Museum can always find some very informative booklets at the information center there.
  參觀國立故宮博物院的旅客們可以在服務中心找到一些資訊豐富的小冊子。

red envelop 名 紅包 （第 24 題）

例句
- Kelly, what are you going to do with your red envelope this year?
  Kelly，妳今年打算怎麼運用妳的紅包錢？

- I look forward to getting red envelopes from my relatives every lunar New Year's Eve.
  每年除夕我都非常期待能收到親戚的紅包。

donate 動 捐獻 （第 24 題）

例句
- I think you should put half of the money in the bank and donate one-third like what we did last year.
  我覺得妳應該把一半的錢存進銀行，並且像我們去年一樣，把三分之一捐出去。

- Richard often donates money to organizations that help animals.
  Richard 常常捐錢給幫助動物的機構。

attraction 名 景點 （第 25 題）

例句
- Yangmingshan National Park has lots of attractions that are worth a visit, such as its hot springs and volcanic landscape.
  陽明山國家公園有許多值得造訪的景點，例如溫泉和火山景觀。

budget 名 預算 （第 25 題）

例句
- Do we need to stay on a tight budget this trip?
  我們這趟旅行的預算很緊嗎？

- Since you have a tight budget for your business trip, book a cheaper hotel.
  既然你出差的預算非常有限，那就訂間便宜的飯店吧。

延伸學習　a tight budget 有限的預算

luxury 名 豪華 （第 25 題）

例句
- I think we can afford a little luxury.
  我們應該可以奢華一點。

- One luxury I always treat myself whenever I go to Thailand is a massage.
  每次造訪泰國我都會奢侈一下享受按摩。

neither...nor 兩者都不 （第 25 題）

例句
- Neither the Express Inn nor the Grand Hotel is close to the city center.
  Express Inn 和 Grand Hotel 離市中心都不近。

- Neither smoking nor drinking is allowed in the theater.
  影廳中禁止抽菸和喝酒。

1. 練習整合圖表與對話內容

生活中常需要一邊聽一邊讀文字或圖表的資訊，例如第 24 題的統計圖、第 25 題的清單、或時刻表等。圖表的資訊和聽到的內容通常相關，但不一定相同。建議平時可利用網路資源，尋找搭配圖表的簡短影音片段，先用幾秒鐘迅速瀏覽圖表重點，例如是關於金額、地點或人名，預測可能的問題，再仔細聆聽對話內容尋找關鍵線索。圖表題需同時用到視覺和聽覺，最怕專注看就忘了聽，或是專注聽就忘了看，所以平時習慣視覺和聽覺雙管齊下，讓注意力可以延伸得更廣，才是提升聽力理解與溝通能力的不二法門。

2. 加強理解言外之意的能力

符號運用與溝通表達包含較迂迴或委婉的表達方式，例如：let someone go 指的是「辭退某人」，between jobs 意思是「目前沒有工作」。平常學習時如果遇到委婉修辭，記得將意思記下以增加印象，也可以多練習參照上下文猜測、判斷訊息間的關聯，推論字面以外的意思。

3. 運用 5W1H 分析法練習深入理解對話內容

平常練習時，利用 5W1H（what、who、where、when、why、how）分析法，掌握對話的主題、說話者身分、發生地點、何時發生、為何發生、如何解決等。

步驟一： 先從整體性的問題著手，對話中最重要的不外乎是主題、人物、地點等，在聽對話前，可以先問 what、who、where 開始的問題，掌握整體的方向，接著聽一遍對話，練習找出答案，以第 22 題為例：

問題	答案
1) **What** are the speakers talking about?	• A custom related to Chinese New Year. • Some strips of paper on the door. • Spring couplets.（春聯）
2) **Who** is the man? 3) **Who** is the woman?	• The man is someone who is not familiar with Chinese customs. • The woman is his friend or his neighbor.
4) **Where** are the speakers?	• They're in front of a house.

步驟二：掌握了整體方向後，可針對細節再想一些問題。第 22 題的主題是春聯，可列一些與春聯相關的問題並找出答案。例如：

問題	答案
5) **When** is the conversation taking place?	• Just before Chinese New Year.
6) **How** long will the strips of paper stay on the door?	• For a year.
7) **Why** does the woman put pieces of paper on the door?	• For good luck.

當然，不是每段對話都可以運用到所有的 5W1H，有時對話發生的地點或人物關係並未明確說明，但練習時可儘量多想一些可能的問題，幫助深入理解對話內容，此練習法不僅適用對話，也可以用在短文的聽解練習。

以上方法只要持之以恆進行，一定能有效提升聽力。

SHORT TALKS

中級聽力
第四部份

簡短談話

聽力測驗 第四部份 簡短談話 New!

這部份每題有一段談話，搭配一個問題，須先正確理解談話內容，再根據問題，選出正確的答案。

本部份評量的學習表現包括：

✓　能聽懂英語簡短談話，並

★　能聽懂情節發展及細節描述

★　能根據上下文釐清訊息

★　能分析、歸納多項訊息

★　能綜合相關資訊預測可能的發展或做合理猜測

★　能理解說話者的觀點、態度與言外之意

考前提醒

這個部份主要評量理解不同類型談話的內容，以及整合歸納重點訊息的能力。談話的種類包含一般的演講、報導、電話留言、公共場所廣播、宣布事項、廣播節目、廣告、簡報、討論及操作說明等。談話內容取材於日常生活、學校生活及職場的情境。

除了前一單元提到的聽解策略外，回答這類型問題時還可運用下列策略。

1. 掌握關鍵資訊

　　當談話篇幅較長或細部資訊較多時，先看選項或圖表可以幫助在聆聽談話時判斷答題需要的重點資訊，聽到問題後再根據這些資訊，推斷出答案。另外，開場和總結都要全神貫注聆聽，說話者通常會開門見山說明主旨，或是在談話最後強調重要結論（例如第34 題）。此外，如果聽到像是 There are three aspects 這樣的句子（例如第 32 題），代表接下來會呈現三個層面的訊息，可以先有心理準備，不要遺漏了。

2. 整合跨句的資訊

　　在談話中關鍵訊息出現後，可能會再以不同的措辭重現於後續內容，可利用這些同義詞確認已知的訊息（例如第 32 題）。另外，答題的相關資訊有時會分散出現於談話中（例如第 26 題），整合這些資訊即可推知正答。

3. 歸納談話要點

　　聆聽時，可將談話的細部資訊依地點、時間、人物、目的等面向歸類（例如第 28 題），有助於完整地理解談話的內容。等聽到問題後，就能很快地找到最適合的選項。

4. 留意問題中的疑問詞或人稱

　　問題所使用的疑問詞（who、where、why 等）或是人稱（the man、the woman、he、she 等）及名稱都是重要的答題線索，要特別留意。

以上答題策略不僅能幫助理解簡短談話的題目，還能培養溝通互動與表達的語言核心能力。

Hello, Caroline. It's Henry. I talked to your mom earlier today, and she told me about the surgery. I've been really worried. I'll come to the hospital to see you sometime tomorrow. Just let me know if you need anything. Hope you get well soon!

哈囉 Caroline，我是 Henry。今天早上我跟妳媽媽聊天，她告訴我妳手術的事。我真的很擔心，如果妳需要什麼跟我說，我明天會去醫院看妳。希望妳早日康復！

What is the purpose of this message?	這個留言的目的是什麼？
A. To offer an apology.	A. 致上歉意
B. To give advice.	B. 給予建議
C. To show admiration.	C. 表示欽佩
D. To express concern.	D. 表達關心

正解 D

本題內容取材自日常的電話留言，需整合歸納留言中的多項訊息，理解說話者交代的前因後果，並判斷說話者的語氣，才能得知這則留言的目的。

說話者一開始先跟 Caroline 解釋如何得知她動手術，直言很擔心她（I've been really worried.），並詢問去探病時要不要順道帶東西給她。留言的最後是個關鍵句，Hope you get well soon!（祝你早日康復）充分表達了說話者的關心，因此可以歸納出本題的正確答案為 D。

關鍵字詞 surgery 手術　worry 擔心

第 27 題

The summer sale is coming! From August 13th to 19th, everything at Jerry's Stationery will be twenty percent off. A free notebook will be given to the first twenty shoppers. More amazing savings will be offered. Hurry up and visit us at 30 Pacific Avenue.

夏季特賣會即將開始！8 月 13 日到 19 日，「Jerry's 文具店」全面八折，前 20 名顧客可獲得免費的筆記本。還有更多好康優惠等著你。快來太平洋大道 30 號。

According to the commercial, how will people get a free notebook?

A. By buying more than twenty items.
B. By shopping with a friend.
C. By making a purchase early.
D. By ordering something online.

根據這則廣告，要怎麼獲得免費筆記本？

A. 買超過二十樣商品
B. 與朋友一起逛街
C. 儘早去購物
D. 線上訂購

正解 C

本題內容取材自日常生活的促銷廣告，需依據關鍵句子的字面意義理解言談，作答時只需聽懂一個關鍵句，便可得知要如何獲得免費贈品。

廣告內容淺顯易懂，訊息包含特賣會的期間和下殺的折扣，但其實只要聽懂關鍵句：A free notebook will be given to the first twenty shoppers.（前 20 名顧客可獲得免費的筆記本）便能得知本題正確答案為 C。

關鍵字詞 purchase 購買

In local news, basketball games for young children will be held at Forest Park this coming Saturday. The organizer of the games, the Southend Community Center, states that children who play team sports are healthier and have better social skills. By holding this event, the center hopes to encourage more children to take up sports.

現在報導國內新聞，本週六兒童籃球賽將於森林公園舉行。賽事主辦單位「Southend 社區中心」表示，參與團體運動的小孩比較健康，而且社交能力較好。藉由舉辦這項活動，中心希望能鼓勵更多孩童運動。

What is said about the event?	關於這項活動，本報導說明了什麼？
A. Why children will love it.	A. 為什麼兒童會喜歡
B. Which teams will show up.	B. 有哪些隊伍會出席
C. What benefits it may bring.	C. 參加有哪些益處
D. How people can sign up.	D. 如何報名參與

正解 C

本題內容取材自簡短的社區新聞報導，綜合上下文的線索，就可以判斷談話的重點。

報導一開始先介紹兒童籃球賽即將在本週末舉行，主辦單位接著表示：**children who play team sports are healthier and have better social skills**（參與團體運動的小孩比較健康，而且社交能力較好），希望藉此鼓勵更多兒童參與。綜合以上線索，可得知本報導主要說明的是參加活動的好處，因此正確答案為 C。

談話會包含很多不同的資訊，平日練習時，可試著將談話中的資訊用簡短的話歸納要點，可以幫助理解談話內容。以本段為例，可先釐清說話者提到的不同資訊是屬於哪些面向，再將內容歸納如下表。作答時可以將歸納的要點與選項比對，找出正確答案。

- **Location**: Forest Park
- **Date**: this Saturday
- **Organizer**: Southend Community Center
- **Benefits of sports**: healthier, better social skills
- **Purpose of the event**: to encourage children to do sports

關鍵字詞 team sport 團體運動　social skill 社交能力、社交技巧　benefit 好處

第 29 題

Our graduation program was held in the college gym. As class leader, I gave a speech. But two minutes after I began speaking, the microphone stopped working. The program director gave me another one, but it didn't work, either. In the end, I had to speak without a microphone. I don't think anyone beyond the third row could hear me.

我們的畢業典禮辦在學校體育館。身為班長，我上台演講，但我才講兩分鐘，麥克風就壞了，司儀給我另一支麥克風也不能用。最後，我只好放棄用麥克風講話，我覺得坐在第三排以後的人應該無法聽見我說的話。

What is the woman saying about her speech?	這位女生在描述演講當時的什麼事情？
A. Her nervous feelings.	A. 她緊張的感覺
B. The response from her audience.	B. 聽眾的回應
C. A short story she told.	C. 她講的故事內容
D. A device problem.	D. 設備的問題

 正解 Ⓓ

本題內容是敘述一位學生於畢業典禮當日所發生的事情。

女生一開始就提到畢業典禮，她上台演講時，**the microphone stopped working** （麥克風壞掉），備用麥克風居然也不能用，所以後排的學生應該都沒有聽到她講話。整段言談主要說明的是她演講當時設備故障的窘境，因此正確答案為 D。

關鍵字詞 microphone 麥克風　device 設備、裝置

Have you all found a partner? Good, let's practice some moves. One of you be the attacker, and the other be the victim. Attacker, grab hold of your partner's right arm. Now victim, turn around and kick your partner in the knee. Lightly, of course. In real situations, you will have to use as much force as you can.

你們都找好搭檔了嗎？好，那我們來練習一些動作。你們其中一個當攻擊的人，另一個當受害者。攻擊者，抓住你搭檔的右手臂。受害者，轉身，然後踢你搭檔的膝蓋。現在當然輕輕地踢就好，但真的遇到的時候，你要用盡全力踢。

What is the speaker teaching?

A. Self-defense.

B. Rock climbing.

C. Dancing.

D. Soccer.

說話者在教什麼？

A. 自我防衛

B. 攀岩

C. 跳舞

D. 足球

正解 A

本題內容取材自一位教練的口頭指導。

從教練的指示：One of you be the attacker, and the other be the victim.（你們其中一個當攻擊的人，另一個當受害者）可以得知這是兩人搭檔的模擬實況練習，之後出現多個關鍵資訊，包括：抓手臂（grab hold of your partner's right arm）、踢膝蓋（kick your partner in the knee）等，合理推論說話者在傳授防身術，因此本題正確答案為 A。

關鍵字詞 attacker 攻擊者　victim 受害者　self-defense 自我防衛

第 31 題

Hi, I'm Nancy, and I'm your guide today. I'm going to take you through the entire area, so you'll be able to see all the animals that we raise, including horses, cows, chickens, and sheep. You'll also have the chance to milk a cow and gather the chickens' eggs. Many of our products, such as milk, cheese, and eggs, are sold at department stores. You can place an order at the end of the tour. Everyone ready to go?

大家好，我是 Nancy，我是你們今天的導遊。我會帶大家逛這整區，讓各位看看我們養的動物，有馬、牛、雞和羊，大家還有機會體驗擠牛奶和撿雞蛋。許多我們的產品像是牛奶、起司和蛋都在百貨公司裡販賣，你們可以在導覽結束時購買。大家準備好要出發了嗎？

Where is the speaker?	說話者在哪裡？
A.　In an aquarium.	A.　在水族館
B.　In a zoo.	B.　在動物園
C.　On a farm.	C.　在農場
D.　At a playground.	D.　在遊樂場

正解 Ⓒ

本題內容取材自一位導遊的行前介紹。

從導遊 Nancy 一開始的介紹可以得知遊客等下會看到多種動物，包括馬、牛、雞和羊等，由此可以初步判斷選項 B：In a zoo.（動物園）或 C：On a farm.（農場）較有可能為本題情境。接著 Nancy 又說 You'll also have the chance to milk a cow and gather the chickens' eggs.（你們有機會體驗擠牛奶和撿雞蛋）這句話排除了動物園的可能性。因此綜合以上線索，本題正確答案為 C。

 milk 擠奶、榨取　gather 收集

The world is facing an environmental crisis that affects every living thing. Thankfully, there are things we can do to address the crisis. We can turn off the lights, avoid using the air conditioner, and take part in recycling projects. These three things can help to cut down the energy we consume. All it takes is a little effort on everyone's part.

世界正在面臨影響所有生物的環境危機。幸好有一些因應的方法，我們可以隨手關燈、避免使用冷氣、進行資源回收。這三件事有助於減少我們消耗的能源，只要每個人都盡一點力就可以挽救環境。

What aspect of the environmental crisis does the speaker focus on?	說話者著重在環境危機的哪個方面？
A. Solutions to it.	A. 解決辦法
B. Public attitudes to it.	B. 大眾的態度
C. The business opportunities.	C. 商機
D. The important causes.	D. 主要原因

 正解 Ⓐ

本題內容取材自一般宣導環保的言談。

男子一開始便說：there are things we can do to address the crisis（有一些因應這些危機的方法），接著舉出三件大家隨手可做的事來提倡環保，最後又強調一次：These three things can help to cut down the energy we consume.（這三件事有助於減少我們消耗的能源），由此可以判斷談話內容著重在因應環境危機的「辦法」，所以 A 為正確答案。

關鍵字詞 environmental crisis 環境危機 recycling 回收 solution 解決辦法

第 33 題

The teacher of my nine-year-old son, William, has a no-homework policy. This means that students are expected to finish their assignment during school hours. There's no extra work for them to bring home. Thanks to this policy, William has time for his hobbies, and we have more family time together.

我九歲兒子 William 的老師有個「零回家作業」的規定，意思是學生應該在學校寫完作業，沒有額外帶回家的作業。多虧這項規定，William 有時間從事他的嗜好，我們一家人也有更多時間相處。

What would the speaker say about the teacher's homework policy?

A. It's not unusual.
B. It should be evaluated.
C. It's quite welcome.
D. It won't have an impact.

說話者是怎麼看老師的作業規定？

A. 很平常
B. 需要評估
C. 很歡迎
D. 沒有影響

 正解 C

本題談話主要談論說話者小孩的學校作業規定，需先理解談話內容，再進一步針對說話者的觀點進行推論與詮釋。

女子一開始便介紹所謂的「零回家作業」規定，並說自己的小孩因而有時間做喜歡做的事，全家人也有更多時間相處。女子接著說明「零回家作業」的好處，從這些線索可以推論她相當支持老師的規定，因此 C 為正確答案。

關鍵字詞 policy 規定、政策　assignment 作業、任務

Participant: Emily Huang	
Judge	**Score given**
Tim Wilson	91
Hugo Davis	95
Frank Taylor	88
Peter Carter	70

參賽者：Emily Huang	
評審	**分數**
Tim Wilson	91
Hugo Davis	95
Frank Taylor	88
Peter Carter	70

For question number 34, please look at the score board.

I was a judge for the English Writing Contest this year. I was careful to follow the rating instructions, but later, when my scores were compared with those of the other three judges, there was a huge difference. For example, this year's champion is Emily Huang, but I wasn't impressed by her performance at all.

關於第 34 題，請看記分板。

我是今年英文寫作比賽的評審。雖然我有認真遵循評分標準，不過我的給分跟其他三位評審相比，差異很大。例如今年的冠軍 Emily Huang，我完全不覺得她的表現哪裡好。

Look at the score board. Who is the speaker?

A. Tim Wilson.
B. Hugo Davis.
C. Frank Taylor.
D. Peter Carter.

請看記分板。說話者是哪位評審？

A. Tim Wilson.
B. Hugo Davis.
C. Frank Taylor.
D. Peter Carter.

正解　D

本題內容是一段與英文寫作比賽相關的談話，需理解並整合言談內容與記分板的訊息，才能推測說話者是哪一位評審。

說話者一開始便表明自己是寫作評審（judge），他以冠軍 Emily 為例說明自己的給分與其他評審差異很大，他最後一句提到：她的作文不怎麼樣（not impressed by her performance），搭配記分表的圖示可以合理推測說話者為給分最低的評審 Peter Carter，因此本題的正確答案為 D。

關鍵字詞　judge 評審、裁判　champion 冠軍　impress （使）感到欽佩、留下好印象

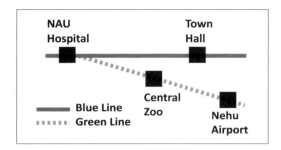 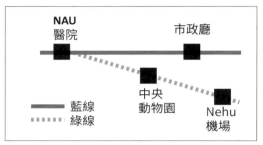

For question number 35, please look at the route map.

Attention ladies and gentlemen. Due to mechanical problems, the Blue Line has suspended service. Passengers who wish to travel to stations on the Blue Line, please take the Green Line or alternative transportation. The City Subway System apologizes for the inconvenience.

關於第 35 題，請看路線圖。

各位先生、女士請注意，由於機械故障，藍線暫時停止服務。想要前往藍線各站的乘客請改搭綠線或其他交通工具。造成您的不便，「城市地鐵」深感抱歉。

Look at the route map. Which station cannot be reached by subway now?

A.   NAU Hospital Station.

B.   Nehu Airport Station.

C.   Central Zoo Station.

D.   Town Hall Station.

請看路線圖。現在搭地鐵無法到達哪一站？

A.   NAU 醫院站

B.   Nehu 機場站

C.   中央動物園站

D.   市政廳站

正解 **D**

本題內容取材自地鐵的廣播公告，需理解並整合言談內容與路線圖的資訊，才能推知正確答案。

站務員廣播的主要內容是藍線停駛，乘客必須改搭綠線。題目問目前無法搭地鐵到哪一站。搭配地鐵路線圖，可以先排除選項 B 和 C 這兩個位於綠線上的車站。至於選項 A：NAU Hospital Station，由於是兩條路線的交會點，搭乘綠線仍可到達，所以也不正確，因此本題的正確答案為 D：Town Hall Station.（市政廳站）。

關鍵字詞 suspend 暫停、使停職

接著我們來複習本部份的重點詞彙

surgery 名 手術 （第 26 題）

例句
- I talked to your mom earlier today, and she told me about the surgery.
  今早我跟妳媽媽聊天，她告訴我妳手術的事。

- My left hand is swollen and the doctor told me I may have to undergo minor surgery.
  我的左手腫腫的，醫生告訴我可能需要做個小手術。

worry 動 擔心 （第 26 題）

例句
- I've been really worried.
  我真的很擔心。

- Mary is worried about giving a speech at the international literature conference.
  對於要在國際文學研討會上發表演說一事，Mary 很擔憂。

延伸學習　be worried about something 擔心某事

purchase 名 購買 （第 27 題）

例句
- This car is the most expensive purchase I've ever made.
  這輛車是我目前買過最貴的東西了。

team sport 團體運動 （第 28 題）

例句
- Children who play team sports are healthier and have better social skills.
  參與團體運動的小孩比較健康，而且社交能力較好。

- Soccer is a team sport that relies heavily on teamwork.
  足球是一種很注重團隊合作的團體運動。

social skill 社交能力、社交技巧 （第 28 題）

例句 • Amanda has such excellent social skills that she was born to be a real estate agent.
Amanda 社交能力非常好，是個天生的房屋仲介。

benefit 名 好處 （第 28 題）

例句 • The benefit of taking these vitamins is that they can prevent some eye diseases.
攝取這些維生素的優點是可以預防眼部疾病。

microphone 名 麥克風 （第 29 題）

例句 • Two minutes after I began speaking, the microphone stopped working.
我上台才演講了兩分鐘，麥克風就壞了。

• This model of microphone is widely used in professional recording studios, for it is very sensitive.
這個型號的麥克風很常被用在專業錄音室，因為它的收音非常細膩。

device 名 設備、裝置 （第 29 題）

例句 • In the 21st century, smartphones have become an indispensable device.
在 21 世紀，智慧型手機已成為一項不可或缺的設備。

attacker 名 攻擊者 （第 30 題）

例句 • One of you be the attacker, and the other be the victim.
你們其中一個當攻擊的人，另一個當受害者。

• There were at least five witnesses claiming that the attacker was wearing a blue shirt.
至少有五個目擊者聲稱他們看到攻擊者身上穿的是一件藍色上衣。

victim 名 受害者 （第 30 題）

例句 • As a victim of the financial crisis in 2008, John went bankrupt and lost his two houses.
John 是 2008 年金融海嘯的受害者，除了破產之外他還損失了兩棟房子。

self-defense 名 自我防衛 （第 30 題）

例句 • The man punched the robber in self-defense.
那位男生出於自我防衛而出手打了那位搶匪。

延伸學習 do something in self-defense 出於自我防衛而做某事

milk 動 擠奶、榨取 （第 31 題）

例句 • You'll have the chance to milk a cow and gather the chickens' eggs.
大家有機會體驗擠牛奶和撿雞蛋。

• The thing I love most about working at a farm is milking the cows every morning.
我在農場最愛的工作就是每天早上幫牛擠牛奶。

gather 動 收集 （第 31 題）

例句 • Before Josh started writing his term paper, he went to the library to gather more information.
Josh 在開始寫期末報告前，先去圖書館收集更多資料。

environmental crisis 環境危機 （第 32 題）

例句 • The world is facing an environmental crisis that affects every living thing.
世界正在面臨一項影響所有生物的環境危機。

• This city is trying to help solve the environmental crisis by planting as many trees as possible and instructing the citizens to save energy.
這個城市正嘗試藉由多種樹跟教導市民如何節約能源來解決環境危機。

recycling 名 回收 （第 32 題）

例句 • We can turn off the lights, avoid using the air conditioner, and take part in recycling projects.
我們可以隨手關燈、避免使用冷氣、進行資源回收。

• Recycling is a government priority.
回收再利用是政府的首要任務。

solution 名 解決辦法 （第 32 題）

例句 • The only solution to this problem is to buy a new printer.
解決這個問題的唯一方法就是買一台新的印表機。

policy 名 規定、政策 （第 33 題）

例句 • Thanks to this policy, William has time for his hobbies, and we have more family time together.
多虧這項規定，William 有時間從事他的嗜好，我們一家人也有更多時間相處。

• The supermarket has relaxed its policy regarding the return of unwanted items.
這間超市鬆綁了他們對於退換貨的規定。

assignment 名 作業、任務 （第 33 題）

例句 • Students are expected to finish their assignment during school hours.
學生應該在學校寫完作業。

• Due to my heavy workload, I need extra time for this assignment.
因為我的工作量太大了，我需要額外的時間來處理這項作業。

judge 名 評審、裁判 （第 34 題）

例句 • I was a judge for the English Writing Contest this year.
我是今年英文寫作比賽的評審。

• Mr. Nicholson has served as a judge for the debate competition for 20 years.
Nicholson 先生已經擔任這個辯論比賽的評審 20 年了。

champion 名 冠軍（第 34 題）

例句
- This year's champion is Emily Huang, but I wasn't impressed by her performance at all.
  今年的冠軍是 Emily Huang，但我完全不覺得她的表現哪裡好。

- Eager to be a champion athlete, Alex practices running every afternoon.
  Alex 很想成為一位冠軍選手，所以他每天下午都在練習跑步。

impress 動 （使）感到欽佩、留下好印象（第 34 題）

例句
- The poet's new work really impressed me by the beauty of his words.
  這位詩人新作品裡的優美文字令我驚豔。

suspend 動 暫停、使停職（第 35 題）

例句
- Due to mechanical problems, the Blue Line has suspended service.
  由於機械故障，藍線暫時停止服務。

- The project has been suspended due to lack of funds.
  這項計畫因為資金短缺的緣故，暫時中止。

Note

1. 廣泛接觸英語媒體

平時多收聽英語廣播或看英文電影、影集等，幫助自己習慣聆聽篇幅稍長的談話，培養語感。英語的學習應該與自己的生活與興趣連結，而非僅是應付考試，因此在選擇聽力音檔或影片時，可先從自己感興趣的主題著手，例如喜歡的影集、感興趣的新聞等，也可訂閱一些國外 YouTuber 的頻道。透過生活中廣泛接觸英語媒體不僅可以增進語言能力，也可以了解多元文化觀點與國際時事，進一步增進多元文化與國際理解的核心素養。

2. 練習掌握關鍵資訊

利用一些可重複播放並附有錄音稿或字幕的音檔與影片，一邊聽一邊記下關鍵字，聽完後，可以利用這些關鍵字回憶剛剛聽的內容，釐清主旨與細節，最後再利用錄音稿或字幕確認自己的理解是否正確。

3. 練習理解圖表

理解圖表的能力是核心素養強調的重要一環，因為在實際生活情境中，圖表隨處可見，因此應該多多練習解讀圖表。首先，看清楚每個座標軸所代表的意義。接著可以試著用英文表達圖表的主題與重要的資訊。反覆地練習，能夠幫助你快速辨識各類圖表重要的資訊。

4. 練習「跟讀」技巧

「跟讀」訓練可以幫助掌握正確發音、加強聽力理解。「跟讀」一詞的英文是 shadowing，即是像影子跟著音檔的說話者複誦。實際上要怎麼練習呢？

(1) 找一個符合自己程度的影片或是音檔。一開始可找一至兩分鐘的影片或音檔，例如本書所附的音檔就很適合，隨著能力越來越進步，再增加音檔長度。

(2) 多聽幾遍音檔，熟悉並理解內容。音檔或影片最好找有附錄音稿或字幕的，對照錄音稿查詢不認識的單字，並完整理解內容。

(3) 在不看錄音稿與字幕的情況下，同步複誦聽到的句子，與說話者之間只有一至兩秒的落差。請跟上說話者的語速，並試著模仿他的發音、重音、語調以及在何處停頓等。同時將自己的練習錄下。

(4) 比較自己的說話方式與音檔說話者的不同之處，再做調整，反覆練習。長久練習後不但可加強聽力，亦可增進口說能力。

總結來說，要加強聽力可以從「量的訓練」以及「質的訓練」這兩大方向加強。主動運用各種學習資源與英語文素材，大量接觸英文，輔以本書提到的學習策略不斷練習，在學習歷程中反覆檢討與改進，英語聽力素養一定會明顯提升！

SENTENCE COMPLETION

閱讀測驗

第一部份

詞彙

閱讀測驗
第一部份 **詞彙**

這部份共有 10 題，每一題均含有一個空格，根據題意選一個最適合的字或詞作答。

本部份評量的學習表現包括：

✓ 能理解常用的詞彙（請參考全民英檢中級字表）
✓ 能掌握詞彙在句子中的用法

考前提醒

這部份評量重點是日常生活中常用的詞彙，考生透過題目所提供的語境線索，選出一個最適合的字或詞來還原題意。考生須能將所學的詞彙應用在題目所提供的情境。

回答這類型的題目時，你可以

1. 掌握關鍵字彙，從情境推論答案

   如果題目中出現不認識的字，不用緊張。因為題目的答題線索通常不只一個，重要的實詞（content words）都可能是幫助解題的關鍵，可以從這些關鍵字推論題目的情境，像是讀到 firefighter（消防員）、trapped（受困）便可聯想到他們的救災工作（rescue）。一旦明確掌握題目的情境，作答能夠更有效率（例如第 1、8、9 題）。

2. 運用語法知識，分析句構理解題意

   遇到較長或句構複雜的題目時，可先分析句構，找出主詞、主要動詞、並掌握子句間的關係，能幫助你理解句意。如果有不認識的字詞，可根據單字在句中的位置判斷其詞性與功能，推論字意（例如第 5、7 題）。

3. 留意完整句意，才不會錯失線索

   閱讀題目時，一定要看完整個句子，才能得知全部的語意與線索，避免誤判（例如第 2、4、10 題）。

字彙、語法、語意是測驗中重要的面向，若能夠加以充實字彙量、熟悉語法，可以有效掌握答題關鍵！

The firefighters are trying to _____ the boy who is trapped in the house that is on fire.

A. rescue

B. defeat

C. propose

D. illustrate

消防員正努力救出受困在著火房子裡的男孩。

A. 救援

B. 打敗

C. 提出

D. 說明

正解 Ⓐ

本題為火災的情境。

本題關鍵字為 firefighter（消防員），其主要任務在救災、救人，且後半句提到 the boy who is trapped in the house that is on fire（受困在著火房子裡的男孩），關係代名詞 who、that 分別修飾男孩和房子，根據題意，只有選項 A：rescue（救援）與情境相符，因此為正確答案。

關鍵字詞 firefighter 消防員 trap 受困 rescue 救援

第 2 題

The nurse will take the patient's blood pressure again because the first reading did not seem to be _____.

A. durable

B. permanent

C. conservative

D. accurate

因為第一次讀數似乎不準，所以護士要再量一次病人的血壓。

A. 耐用的

B. 永久性的

C. 保守的

D. 準確的

正解 D

本題是醫院裡護士量血壓的情境，仔細看完整句的資訊，掌握題意中的「因果關係」才能選答。

本題的句子內容分析如下：

主要子句 「結果」	The nurse will take the patient's blood pressure again
從屬子句 「原因」	**because** the first reading did not seem to be _____.

題目是一個連接詞 because（因為）連接的兩個子句。Because 用於陳述因果關係，常見語法為「結果 + because + 原因」；題意為 the first reading did not seem to be _____（第一次讀數似乎 ___）導致 The nurse will take the patient's blood pressure again（護士要再量一次病人的血壓）。四個選項中，只有 D：accurate（準確的）可形容數值或刻度的準確性，且還原題意的因果關係，因此為正確答案。

其他選項 durable 用來形容物品的耐用度，permanent 形容事、物永恆不變的特性，conservative 形容人的態度保守或物品樣式不夠新穎，都不符合題意。

關鍵字詞 blood pressure 血壓　reading 讀數　accurate 準確的

Dressing _____ is a simple but effective way to make a favorable initial impression.

A. clumsily

B. properly

C. hurriedly

D. beneficially

穿著得體是給人留下良好第一印象簡單卻有效的方法。

A. 笨拙地

B. 適當地

C. 匆忙地

D. 受益地

正解 B

本題為對一般社交穿著的建議。

句子後半段提到 make a favorable initial impression（給人留下良好的第一印象），可推測前半句的用語是較正面的意思，選項 B：properly（適當地）和 D：beneficially（受益地）中，只有前者搭配 dressing，語意才適切，故為正確答案。

關鍵字詞 initial 最初的 impression 印象 properly 適當地

第 4 題

Mom often divides household
_____, such as doing the dishes
or taking out the trash, among my
brothers and me.

A. goods

B. expenses

C. chores

D. appliances

媽媽常分派家事，像洗碗或倒垃圾，給我和
哥哥弟弟做。

A. 貨物

B. 費用

C. 雜務

D. 家用電器

正解 C

本題取材自家庭生活情境。

從 such as（例如）後出現的 do the dishes（洗碗）和 take out the trash（倒垃圾），判斷空格裡需要的字是家裡的雜務，只有選項 C 和 household 搭配為 household chores（家庭雜務）符合題意，因此為正確答案。

關 鍵 字 詞 household chore 家庭雜務

After _____ the dust that had long covered the old photograph, Jack was finally able to identify the people in it.

Jack 擦去長久覆蓋在老照片上的灰塵後，終於能認出裡頭的人。

A.　handing over

B.　wiping away

C.　snapping off

D.　rising up

A.　交出

B.　擦去

C.　折斷

D.　升起

正解 B

本題取材自日常生活情境。

本題的句構分析如下：

After + V-ing	After _____ the dust （在 _____ 灰塵後）
that 引導的關係子句形容 dust	that had long covered the old photograph,（長久覆蓋在老照片上）
主要句子	Jack was finally able to identify the people in it.（Jack 終於能認出裡頭的人。）

此句的關鍵句型是 After + V₁-ing, S + V₂，此句構等同於 After S + V₁, S + V₂，因此前半句的主詞也是 Jack，本題須從後方句意推論 Jack 做了什麼事後，才能看清照片。題目前半段提及 the dust that had long covered the old photograph（長久覆蓋在老照片上的灰塵），就語意上，「擦拭、清除」灰塵後才能看清照片，只有選項 B：wiping away 表示這樣的動作，因此為正確答案。

關鍵字詞 wipe away 擦去、清除　dust 灰塵　identify 辨認

第 6 題

In order to better manage his allowance, Scott has decided to record his daily expenses _____.

A. in return

B. back and forth

C. from now on

D. behind the times

為了好好支配零用錢，Scott 決定從現在開始記錄日常開銷。

A. 作為回報

B. 一來一往

C. 從現在開始

D. 過時的

正解 C

本題取材自日常生活情境。

本題先說明 in order to better manage his allowances（為了好好支配零用錢），在這個前提下，Scott 才決定要記錄他每天的花費，根據語意，只有選項 C：from now on（從現在開始）符合前後邏輯，故為正確答案。

關鍵字詞 allowance 零用錢　record 記錄　expense 費用、花費

Steve's desire to play on the school basketball team has _____ him to practice every day.

A. explored
B. motivated
C. composed
D. organized

Steve 想進籃球校隊的願望激勵著他每天練球。

A. 探索
B. 激勵
C. 組成
D. 安排

正解 B

本題取材自校園情境。

句子較長,可以透過分析句構幫助掌握句意。

主詞	Steve's desire to play on the school basketball team
動詞	has _____
受詞	him
不定詞補語	to practice every day.

Steve 每天練球的原因是 Steve's desire to play on the school basketball team(Steve 想進籃球校隊),desire(渴望)可以促使一個人積極地從事某件事。四個選項中,唯有 motivate 有激發人的意思,因此正確答案為 B。

關鍵字詞 motivate 激勵、使產生動機

第 8 題

The ＿＿＿＿＿＿ for Sandy's business trip will be arranged by her company.

A. accommodation

B. representation

C. inspiration

D. expectation

Sandy 出差的住宿將由公司安排。

A. 住宿

B. 代表

C. 靈感

D. 期待

正解 Ⓐ

本題取材自職場情境。

題目說明公司安排出差（**business trip**）的事項，一般而言，旅行前都會事先安排好「交通」和「住宿」，選項中，只有 accommodation（住宿）與情境相符，因此正確答案為 A。

關鍵字詞 business trip 商務旅行、出差　arrange 安排　accommodation 住宿

If you want to write a good science paper, you must provide enough _____ and use it effectively to support your argument.

A. significance

B. occupation

C. endurance

D. evidence

想寫好一篇理科論文，就必須提出充分的證據，並有效運用它來支持論點。

A. 重要性

B. 職業

C. 忍耐

D. 證據

正解 D

本題取材自學術情境。

本句的關鍵句型是用連接詞 if 引導的一般條件句。根據題意，寫好一篇理科論文（science paper）的先決條件是 provide enough _____（提出充分的 _____）和 use it effectively to support your argument（有效運用它來支持論點），邏輯上，與論證有關的字詞只有選項 D：evidence（證據），因此正確答案為 D。

關鍵字詞 evidence 證據 argument 論點

第 10 題

Do not skip meals anymore; _____ eating may harm your stomach.

A. practical
B. vegetarian
C. irregular
D. essential

別再不吃飯了，飲食不規律可能會傷胃。

A. 實際的
B. 素食的
C. 不規律的
D. 必要的

正解 C

本題內容為一般的健康概念。

題目前半段 Do not skip meals anymore（別再不吃飯了）為重點提示。有一餐沒一餐的，表示飲食不規律，四個選項中，只有 irregular（不規律的）和頻率有關，因此正確答案為 C。選項 B：vegetarian（素食的）雖然和飲食相關，但和前一句的語意不符。

關鍵字詞 skip 跳過、略過　irregular 不規律的、不規則的

關鍵字詞

接著我們來複習本部份的重點詞彙

firefighter 名 消防員（第 1 題）

例句 • The firefighters are trying to rescue the boy who is trapped in the house that is on fire.
消防員正努力救出受困在著火房子裡的男孩。

• Warren decided to become a firefighter when he was saved by one as a child.
自從小時候消防員救了 Warren 一命後，他便決定要成為消防員。

trap 動 受困（第 1 題）

例句 • Few hours after wandering away from its owner, the dog was found trapped in a sewer.
跟主人走散幾個小時後，這隻狗狗被發現受困在下水道中。

rescue 動 救援（第 1 題）

例句 • The soldier rescued the victims after the typhoon destroyed their village.
颱風侵襲村落後，軍人前來救援受災戶。

blood pressure 血壓（第 2 題）

例句 • The nurse will take the patient's blood pressure again because the first reading did not seem to be accurate.
因為第一次讀數似乎不準，所以護士要再量一次病人的血壓。

• Patients suffering from high blood pressure need to take medicine and eat a healthy diet.
罹患高血壓的病患必須服藥和維持健康飲食。

reading 名 讀數（第 2 題）

例句 • After the reading on a scale displayed the weight, the boxing contestant was quite shocked.
磅秤顯示體重讀數後，拳擊選手非常吃驚。

accurate 形 準確的（第 2 題）

例句 • My watch does not tell the accurate time, so I need to change its battery.
我手錶的時間不準了，所以我需要換電池。

initial 形 最初的（第 3 題）

例句 • Dressing properly is a simple but effective way to make a favorable initial impression.
穿著得體是給人留下良好第一印象簡單卻有效的方法。

• The student's initial reaction to the cancellation of the math test was relief.
學生對於數學考試取消的第一反應是鬆了口氣。

impression 名 印象（第 3 題）

例句 • I had a positive impression about the campus, and later decided to study there.
我對這個校園印象很好，而後決定要在此就學。

properly 副 適當地（第 3 題）

例句 • Managers need to control the budget properly; otherwise, they may have difficulty completing the projects.
主管們需要適當地控制預算，否則，他們要完成計畫會有困難。

household chore 家庭雜務（第 4 題）

例句 • Mom often divides household chores, such as doing the dishes or taking out the trash, among my brothers and me.
媽媽常分派家事，像洗碗或倒垃圾，給我和哥哥弟弟做。

• My roommate helps with household chores like mopping the floor and watering the plants.
我室友幫忙做像是拖地和澆花的家事。

wipe away 擦去、清除（第 5 題）

例句
- After wiping away the dust that had long covered the old photograph, Jack was finally able to identify the people in it.
  Jack 擦去長久覆蓋在老照片上的灰塵後，終於能認出裡頭的人。

- Patty secretly wiped her tears away before anyone noticed.
  在其他人發現之前，Patty 偷偷擦去淚水。

dust 名 灰塵（第 5 題）

例句
- Returning from a two-month road trip, I found the furniture in my apartment covered with dust.
  自為期兩個月的公路旅行返家，我發現公寓裡的家具佈滿灰塵。

identify 動 辨認（第 5 題）

例句
- The police cannot identify the suspect because he had plastic surgery.
  這位警察無法辨識嫌疑犯，因為他曾經整容。

allowance 名 零用錢（第 6 題）

例句
- In order to better manage his allowance, Scott has decided to record his daily expenses from now on.
  為了好好支配零用錢，Scott 決定從現在開始記錄日常開銷。

- Tom spent most of the allowance his parents gave him on toy cars this month.
  這個月，Tom 把父母給的零用錢幾乎全花在玩具車上。

record 動 記錄（第 6 題）

例句
- To record my life, I take photos and then post them on my Instagram account.
  我拍照然後發布在我的 Instagram 帳號來記錄生活。

expense 名 費用、花費（第 6 題）

例句
- When we travel overseas to exhibit our products, the company will cover our transportation expenses.
  公司會支付我們在國外展示產品的交通花費。

motivate **動** 激勵、使產生動機（第 7 題）

例句 • Steve's desire to play on the school basketball team has motivated him to practice every day.
Steve 想進籃球校隊的願望激勵著他每天練球。

• By sharing her own experience of writing novels, the lecturer motivated the students to expand their imagination .
這位講師分享她自身寫小說的經驗，來鼓勵學生發揮想像力。

business trip 商務旅行、出差（第 8 題）

例句 • The accommodation for Sandy's business trip will be arranged by her company.
Sandy 出差的住宿將由公司安排。

• Since the director is on a business trip, her incoming calls will be transferred to her secretary.
因為主任出差中，她的來電會被轉接到祕書那裡。

arrange **動** 安排（第 8 題）

例句 • Our teacher arranged a field trip to the west coast so that we can tour several universities there.
我們的老師安排了到西岸的校外旅行，讓我們可以參訪幾所那邊的大學。

accommodation **名** 住宿（第 8 題）

例句 • Many summer camps provide accommodations so the participants do not need to return home each evening.
很多夏令營提供住宿，所以參加者不需要每天傍晚回家。

evidence **名** 證據（第 9 題）

例句 • If you want to write a good science paper, you must provide enough evidence and use it effectively to support your argument.
想寫好一篇理科論文，就必須提出充分的證據，並有效運用它來支持論點。

• The fingerprint matching evidence indicates that the man was wronged, and more time will be required to find the real criminal.
指紋配對證明顯示這個人被冤枉，要找出真正的罪犯還需要更多時間。

argument 名 論點（第 9 題）

例句 • This presidential candidate summarized his arguments with figures and examples.
這位總統候選人用圖表和例子總結他的論點。

skip 動 跳過、略過（第 10 題）

例句 • Do not skip meals anymore; irregular eating may harm your stomach.
別再不吃飯了，飲食不規律可能會傷胃。

• Anyone that skips the class more than three times is likely to fail the course.
任何人缺課超過三次都有可能無法通過這門課。

irregular 形 不規律的、不規則的（第 10 題）

例句 • The piece of wood has an irregular shape, which makes it hard to make it into a table.
這塊木頭形狀不規則，因此很難做成桌子。

Note

1. 透過熟悉的情境與句構練習造句，加強字彙練習

每當學到一個新的詞彙或片語時，除了閱讀其字典上的定義，也可以試著套用熟悉的句型或新學會的句構練習造句。舉例來說，如剛學到 fall asleep 這個片語，可將其融入生活情境造句，像是 I fell asleep as soon as I crawled into my bed.（我一爬上床就睡著了） 或是 I couldn't help falling asleep in math class.（上數學課時，我忍不住睡著了。）等。透過這樣的練習，不僅加深對句型與字義的理解，也讓學習更為主動，強化自主學習，不再只是死記句型。

2. 以主題與類別有系統地擴充單字量

一篇文章、段落、甚至一個句子中所出現的單字絕不是毫無相關、各自獨立的。文章中出現的單字通常是與文章主題相關的詞彙。我們在學習新單字時可以同時擴充與情境及主題相似的詞彙。例如當我們讀到 firefighter（消防員），可以統整相關的字彙，像是 accident（意外）、緊急事件（emergency）、first aid（急救）等，還可以進一步以「類型、程度」為標準，繼續擴充同主題的字詞量。例如從「災害」的種類，我們可以延伸記下 storm（暴風雨）、earthquake（地震）、fire（火災）、trapped animal（動物受困）；與消防工作有關的器具，可以聯想到 extinguisher（滅火器）、siren（警報器）、fire drill（防火演練）等。日後如果讀到相關主題的其他文章，當中出現跟這個主題高度相關的單字，就可以持續擴充詞彙量，這麼做也有助於提升閱讀速度。

3. 學習搭配詞與片語的正確用法

片語和搭配詞在人際溝通互動與表達上也扮演重要角色。片語多是由二至三個字組成，像是 dress up（盛裝打扮）或是 take place（發生），搭配詞則是常見的字詞組合，像是 vote for（投票支持）、vote against（投票反對）、form a habit（養成習慣）等。這些字的組合經常一起出現，如果寫錯一個部份，譬如將 dress up 寫成 dress over，就無法正確表達。平日學習遇到搭配詞和片語時，可以參考字典中的例句、也可以在閱讀文章時觀察作者的使用方式，才能學習道地的表達方式。

平時累積字彙量，同時兼顧片語、文法的學習，不僅可以提升閱讀力，對寫作能力也很有幫助。

CLOZE

段落填空

這部份有兩個段落，每個段落中有數個空格，須根據文意、句構、上下文邏輯從選項中選出最適合題意的字詞或句子，以還原文章。

本部份評量的學習表現包括：

- ✓ 能理解常用的詞彙（請參考全民英檢中級字表）
- ✓ 能掌握詞彙的用法和語法的規則
- ✓ 能利用字詞結構、上下文意、句型及篇章組織推測詞彙或句子意思

考前提醒

這部份評量重點除了常用詞彙與語法結構外，還包括理解文章的脈絡與前後句子的邏輯關係。考生需能在較長篇幅的語境脈絡下，將所學詞彙應用於題目中的情境，選出最能銜接句子且與文意連貫的選項。

回答這類型的題目時，你可以

1. 了解連接詞與轉折詞的用法，釐清上下文邏輯關係

閱讀時，特別留意連接詞與轉折詞，例如：but、after、as soon as、then、however、unfortunately、in addition 等。這些詞彙可以加強文章的連貫性，有時也用來表示語氣或是文意的轉變，掌握這些連接詞與轉折詞的用法，可以幫助你整理文章的脈絡（例如第 15、19 題）。

2. 熟悉英文文章維持語意連貫的方式

文章中通常會使用不同的字詞，重複闡述意見或概念，加強整體的連貫性。例如：The program provides online courses that have been approved for credits.（這計畫提供有學分的線上課程）Doing so motivates the students to contribute more to the discussion.（這麼做鼓勵學生更投入討論），Doing so 指的是上句提及的「提供有學分的線上課程」。在第二個題組中也可以看到這個寫作機制（例如：第 17 題的 the annoying behavior 後面改用 this problem）。理解這樣的連貫性特點，不但閱讀英文文章時，可以更精準找出上下文語意關係，對提升寫作能力也有很大的幫助。

3. 確實掌握代名詞的用法

為避免累贅，英文文章中常用代名詞，替代前文提及的人、事、物，行文也會比較流暢。確實了解每個代名詞在段落中所代替的詞彙，可以幫助釐清上下文的語意邏輯，才能正確理解文意（例如第 11、15、20 題）。

透過以上技巧，可以減少閱讀理解過程中可能遇到的困難，順利推敲正解！

Jason had imagined himself going skydiving ever since he was a child. Last Saturday, for his twentieth birthday, he finally _(11)_ . His parents generously paid for him to take lessons from a qualified _(12)_ , Sherry Black. On the morning of Jason's birthday, Sherry introduced to Jason the equipment they needed and explained the best way to use it. She then _(13)_ how to jump out of the plane and land safely. After lunch, she and Jason went up in a small plane _(14)_ a pilot. When they reached a height of 4,000 meters, Sherry and Jason jumped out of the plane and then quickly opened their parachutes. _(15)_ , they drifted slowly to the ground. Jason had a wonderful time and is looking forward to a new adventure on his next birthday.

本段落為一篇敘述文，內容描述 Jason 在二十歲生日時的跳傘體驗。

第 11 題　　New!

A. experienced what it was really like

A. 體驗跳傘真正的滋味

B. invited his friends to his birthday party

B. 邀請朋友們去他的生日派對

C. had the courage to ask a girl out

C. 鼓起勇氣約女生出去

D. got his license to fly an airplane

D. 拿到開飛機的執照

正解 A

本題評量文意連貫性。作答時需從空格前、後的句子找出字詞的連貫性，同時需理解代名詞 it 所指稱的對象，才能判斷最符合文章邏輯發展的選項。

空格前後內容分析如下：

前一句	Jason had imagined himself going skydiving ever since he was a child.（Jason 從小就一直想去跳傘。）
空格句	Last Saturday, for his twentieth birthday, he finally ＿＿＿.（上星期六，為了慶祝他的二十歲生日，他終於 ＿＿＿ 。）
後一句	His parents generously paid for him to take lessons from a qualified instructor, Sherry Black.（Jason 的父母慷慨地付費讓他找合格的教練 Sherry Black 上課。）

統整這幾句的關鍵資訊（skydiving, birthday, lessons）後可推知，空格句的句意應與體驗跳傘有關，語意才會連貫，選項 A 中的 it 所指稱的是前一句所提到的 skydiving，因此正確答案是 A：experienced what it was really like（體驗跳傘真正的滋味），其他選項僅與生日相關，但是語意並不符合前後句的邏輯關係。

關鍵字詞 go skydiving 跳傘

A.　spectator
B.　ambassador
C.　instructor
D.　competitor

A.　旁觀者、觀眾
B.　大使
C.　教練
D.　競爭者

正解 Ⓒ

本題評量名詞的語意與用法。需釐清上下文語意與每個選項的字義，並參考搭配詞用法，才能找出最符合文意的答案。

空格的前面提到 His parents generously paid for him to take lessons（Jason 的父母慷慨地付費讓他上課），而且是一位合格的（qualified）人士，四個選項中，只有 C：instructor（教練）的工作是在上課，且可以跟 qualified 搭配使用，故為正確答案。

關鍵字詞 take lessons 上課　instructor 教練、教師

第 13 題

A. implemented	A. 執行
B. demonstrated	B. 演示、展示
C. expanded	C. 擴張
D. attempted	D. 嘗試

正解 Ⓑ

本題評量動詞的語意與用法。只要理解上下文語意，釐清文中所描述的一連串動作的順序，就不難選出答案。

空格句與前方句子內容分析如下：

前一句	Sherry introduced to Jason the equipment they needed and explained the best way to use it. （Sherry 向 Jason 介紹他們所需的裝備，還解釋最佳操作方式。）
空格句	She then ＿＿＿＿ how to jump out of the plane and land safely. （接著她 ＿＿＿＿ 如何跳下飛機並安全地著陸。）

從空格前一句我們知道 Sherry 在介紹跳傘裝備。而從空格前方的副詞 then（然後）可判斷上下兩句是相連的動作，只有選項 B：demonstrate（演示、展示）符合上下文語意。選項 A 的語意雖然也是可能答案，但是在閱讀後兩句後可得知，他們尚未登上飛機，故目前教練僅先示範，尚未實際執行。而選項 C 與 D 的語意皆不相符。

關鍵字詞 introduce 介紹　explain 說明　then 然後　demonstrate 演示、展示

A. with	A. 和、有…的
B. to	B. 到、朝著
C. of	C. 屬於…的
D. upon	D. 在上面、當…時候

正解 Ⓐ

本題評量能否掌握介係詞 with 的語法規則。

根據語意，Jason 和教練登上一架「有飛行員駕駛的」小飛機，只有 with（和、有…的）的語意與用法皆相符，正解為 A。

第 15 題

A. Nevertheless	A. 然而
B. At first	B. 起初
C. Particularly	C. 特別是
D. After that	D. 在那之後

正解 Ⓓ

回答本題時，必須了解上下文關係，掌握文章的連貫性以及代名詞指稱的對象，就能判斷最符合文章邏輯發展的選項。

空格句與前方句子內容分析如下：

前一句	When they reached a height of 4,000 meters, Sherry and Jason jumped out of the plane and then quickly opened their parachutes.（當 Sherry 和 Jason 飛到 4,000 公尺高時，他們跳下飛機並很快地打開降落傘。）
空格句	_____, they drifted slowly to the ground.（ _____，他們慢慢飄向地面。）

這兩個句子描述了整個跳傘的過程，因此為了讓這兩句可以更連貫，應該加入一個與時間、動作順序相關的連接詞或轉折詞。選項中只有選項 B、D 適用於時間、動作順序，而空格所在是緊接前一句的動作，因此只有 D：After that（在那之後）相符，that 在此作代名詞用，替代前面整句。

關 鍵 字 詞　after that 在那之後　at first 起初

接下來讓我們複習本部份的重點詞彙

go skydiving 跳傘（第 11 題）

例句
- Jason had imagined himself going skydiving ever since he was a child.
  Jason 從小就一直想去跳傘。

- My wife and I went skydiving once when we were on our honeymoon.
  我和我太太在蜜月旅行時曾去跳傘。

take lessons 上課（第 12 題）

例句
- His parents generously paid for him to take lessons from a qualified instructor, Sherry Black.
  Jason 的父母慷慨地付費讓他找合格教練 Sherry Black 上課。

- As an international student, Annie has to take lessons in Chinese speaking and writing.
  身為國際學生，Annie 要上中文口說和寫作課程。

instructor 名 教練、教師（第 12 題）

例句
- The instructor assigned three readings to his students and asked them to hand in their summaries next week.
  這位教師指定他的學生閱讀三篇文章，並要求他們下週繳交摘要。

introduce 動 介紹（第 13 題）

例句
- On the morning of Jason's birthday, Sherry introduced to Jason the equipment they needed and explained the best way to use it.
  在 Jason 生日那天的早上，Sherry 向 Jason 介紹他們所需的裝備，還解釋最佳操作方式。

- In the art museum, the staff member introduced how the past events influenced the painter's style.
  在美術館，館員介紹過去事件如何影響這位畫家的風格。

explain 動 說明（第 13 題）

例句 • She then demonstrated how to jump out of the plane and land safely.
接著她示範如何跳下飛機並安全地著陸。

• Although the mother explained to her son the reason why they had to move, he was still upset.
雖然這位母親向兒子解釋必須搬家的原因，他仍然很難過。

then 副 然後（第 13 題）

例句 • Register for the marathon online, and then transfer the fee to the account below.
上網報名馬拉松，然後轉帳報名費到以下帳戶。

demonstrate 動 演示、展示（第 13 題）

例句 • The teacher first introduced the different parts of the microscope and then demonstrated how to use it.
老師先介紹了顯微鏡的各個構造，接著示範如何使用。

after that 在那之後（第 15 題）

例句 • After that, they drifted slowly to the ground.
在那之後，他們慢慢飄向地面。

• He worked as a project manager in a travel agency; after that, he took over his father's business.
他在一家旅行社擔任專案經理，在那之後，他接管了他父親的事業。

at first 起初（第 15 題）

例句 • At first, the successful businessman turned down our invitation to speak at our conference, but he was persuaded to do so two months later.
起初，那名成功的企業家拒絕我們研討會演講的邀約，但兩個月後他被說服出席了。

Certain high-pitched sounds can be heard by youngsters but not by adults. An inventor in England has applied this knowledge to a device called the Mosquito, which is intended to keep young trouble-makers away from stores by   (16) . Some shops in England have complained about the   (17)   behavior of teenage gangs who gather nearby and scare customers away. One solution to this problem is to   (18)   a Mosquito near the front door.   (19)   teenage gangs come around, the painful sound that the machine makes will force them to leave. Of course, the Mosquito may also   (20)   other young customers. But this isn't a serious problem for shops that mainly sell products to adults.

本段落為一篇說明文,內容說明一名英國發明家利用「某些高音頻的聲音只有青少年聽得到」的原理發明一種裝置,幫助商店擺脫少年結群鬧事的困擾。

第 16 題　New!

A. producing an awful buzz
B. putting up a warning sign
C. sprinkling water on them
D. releasing harmful insects

A. 發出可怕的嗡嗡聲
B. 張貼警告標語
C. 在他們身上灑水
D. 放出害蟲

正解 Ⓐ

本題評量文意連貫性。需釐清上下文關係，根據語境推敲含意，才能判斷符合邏輯的詞意。

段落一開始即說明 Certain high-pitched sounds can be heard by youngsters（某些高音頻的聲音只有青少年聽得到），並在倒數第三句提到 the painful sound that the machine makes will force them to leave（機器發出的刺耳聲會驅離他們），四個選項中，只有選項 A 與聲音（sound）有關，因此為正確答案。

關鍵字詞 high-pitched 高音的　sound 聲音　device 裝置

A. competitive   A. 競爭的

B. annoying   B. 討厭的

C. responsible   C. 盡責的

D. forgetful   D. 健忘的

正解 B

本題評量形容詞的語意與用法。答題時需釐清上下文關係，並根據語意推敲最適合的形容詞。

空格句與後方句子內容分析如下：

空格句	Some shops in England have complained about the _____ behavior of teenage gangs who gather nearby and scare customers away.（英國有些商店抱怨少年在附近聚集而嚇跑客人的 _____ 行為。）
後一句	One solution to this problem is to install a Mosquito near the front door.（解決這個問題的其中一個方式是把 Mosquito 安裝在靠近前門的地方。）

從空格句提到的 complained（抱怨）和 scare（使…驚嚇、把…嚇跑）兩個字，可推知空格內可能是偏負面的形容詞。而後一句的 this problem 指的是前一句少年在店家附近成群結黨的行為，既然作者認為他們的行為是一種「問題」，因此可得知，最符合句意的只有選項 B：annoying（討厭的）。

關 鍵 字 詞 complain 抱怨　scare 使…驚嚇、把…嚇跑　annoying 討厭的、惱人的

第 18 題

A. access

B. observe

C. install

D. affect

A. 接近

B. 觀察

C. 安裝

D. 影響

正解 Ⓒ

本題評量動詞的語意與用法。需要釐清上下文關係，並留意前文闡述的概念，才能選出最適合此句的動詞。

本句 One solution to this problem is to _____ a Mosquito near the front door. 句意為：解決青少年鬧事的方法是把 Mosquito _____ 在靠近前門的地方，而本文第二句已提到 Mosquito 是一種 device（裝置），而非原本的字意「蚊子」，因此，動詞 install（安裝）才是正確答案。

關鍵字詞 install 安裝

A. As soon as   A. 一…就…

B. Even so   B. 即使如此

C. Unless   C. 除非

D. Despite   D. 無論、儘管

正解 Ⓐ

本題評量連接詞的語意和用法。需釐清上下文關係，才能選出最適合的連接詞。

此句的關鍵句型是從屬連接詞 as soon as 所引導的從屬子句，只要掌握這個連接詞的語意與用法，就可判斷正確答案。

空格句與前方句子內容分析如下：

前一句	One solution to this problem is to install a Mosquito near the front door. （解決這個問題的其中一個方式是把 Mosquito 安裝在前門附近。）
空格句	＿＿＿ teenage gangs come around, the painful sound that the machine makes will force them to leave. （＿＿＿ 結群的少年靠近，機器就會發出刺耳聲驅離他們。）

空格前一句的語意是「把 Mosquito 這個裝置安裝在前門附近」，而空格句補充說明「少年結群靠近時，機器會發出刺耳聲」，綜合兩句的語意可推論最適合此處的連接詞應該要與「時間」相關（例如：when、after、as soon as 等），因此選項 A：As soon as（一…就…）是最合適的答案。其他選項的語意與此情境不符。

關鍵字詞 as soon as 一…就… painful 令人痛苦的

第 20 題

A.　tolerate

B.　discourage

C.　withdraw

D.　remove

A.　容忍

B.　阻撓

C.　退出

D.　去除

正解 B

本題評量動詞的語意與用法。必須充分理解前後句意與代名詞指稱的事物，並釐清各選項字義的差別，才能選出正確答案。

空格句與後方句子內容分析如下：

空格句	Mosquito may also _____ other young customers.（Mosquito 這個裝置可能同時會 _____ 其他年輕客群）
後一句	But **this** isn't a serious problem for shops that mainly sell products to adults.（但這對於以成年人為主要客群的商店來說，並非什麼大問題。）

首先要先釐清空格後一句的代名詞 this 指的正是空格句所提到的 Mosquito 這個裝置會帶來的後果，而這個後果對於以成人為主客群的商店來說不是什麼大問題，綜合以上線索可推論空格句的句意應是「Mosquito 這個裝置可能同時使年輕客群卻步，不上門消費」，選項 B 最符合文意。

選項 A 與文意不符，選項 C、D 雖然都含有「無法前進」的意思，但是選項 C：withdraw 通常用在某人自動退出某個情境、選項 D：remove 指的是免除某人的職務，兩者和上下文邏輯不符，因此不是正確答案。

關鍵字詞 discourage 阻撓

接著我們來複習本部份的重點詞彙

high-pitched 形 高音的（第 16 題）

例句
- Certain high-pitched sounds can be heard by youngsters but not by adults.
  某些高音頻的聲音只有青少年聽得到，而成人聽不到。

- Shorter and lighter strings of the piano produce high-pitched notes.
  較短、較輕的鋼琴琴弦能發出高音。

sound 名 聲音（第 16 題）

例句
- My sister complained about the old air conditioner making sounds at night.
  我姐姐抱怨老舊冷氣機晚上會發出噪音。

device 名 裝置（第 16 題）

例句
- An inventor in England has applied this knowledge to a device called the Mosquito, which is intended to keep young trouble-makers away from stores by producing an awful buzz.
  一名英國的發明家將這個原理應用在一種被稱為 Mosquito 的裝置，可發出可怕的嗡嗡聲好讓這些年輕的麻煩製造者遠離店家。

- The GPS device showed the missing ship's location, which helped the navy to locate it quickly.
  那台全球衛星定位系統裝置顯示了失蹤船隻的位置，幫助海軍快速確定它的地點。

complain 動 抱怨（第 17 題）

例句
- Some shops in England have complained about the annoying behavior of teenage gangs who gather nearby and scare customers away.
  英國有些商店抱怨少年在附近成群結黨，而嚇跑客人的惱人行為。

- After waiting thirty minutes for his food to be served, the man complained to the manager.
  這男人等了三十分鐘，食物還沒上桌，於是向經理抱怨。

scare **動** 使…驚嚇、把…嚇跑（第 17 題）

例句 • My neighbor's extremely serious face scares people, but in fact, she has a kind heart.
我鄰居嚴肅的臉很嚇人，但事實上，她有一顆善良的心。

annoying **形** 討厭的、惱人的（第 17 題）

例句 • The secretary found her constant coughing annoying, so she kept drinking hot water.
這位秘書覺得自己不斷咳嗽很惱人，所以一直喝熱水。

install **動** 安裝（第 18 題）

例句 • One solution to this problem is to install a Mosquito near the front door.
解決青少年鬧事的一個方法是把 Mosquito 安裝在前門附近。

• You can install the bus application, so you won't have to wait at a bus stop for too long.
你可以安裝這個公車應用程式，如此就不用在公車站牌等太久。

as soon as 一…就…（第 19 題）

例句 • As soon as teenage gangs come around, the painful sound that the machine makes will force them to leave.
當少年結群靠近，機器就會發出刺耳聲驅離他們。

• As soon as the guest entered the lobby, the hotel staff welcomed him with a big smile.
這位客人一進到大廳，飯店人員就以大大的微笑歡迎他。

painful **形** 令人痛苦的（第 19 題）

例句 • The injection was so painful that the baby burst out crying.
打針非常疼痛，使得這個嬰兒嚎啕大哭。

discourage **動** 阻撓（第 20 題）

例句 • A failed business did not discourage Mr. Chang from starting a new company.
一次失敗的生意經驗並沒有阻撓張先生開設一家新公司。

1. **依據語意分類學習連接詞、轉折詞，幫助釐清上下文邏輯關係**

   閱讀文章時，留意作者所使用的連接詞與轉折詞，分析辨別它的語意，再依照類別記下這些詞彙，例如「與時間相關」的詞彙有 while、meanwhile、as soon as 等；欲「進一步說明」時用 in other words、to put it differently 等；說明結果則常用 as a result、for that reason 等。這些系統性思考的能力，可以幫助你在閱讀時迅速掌握前後句子的關係、加速釐清文章的論述邏輯、提升閱讀理解素養。

2. **觀察文章的組織與連貫性**

   好的文章一定有好的連貫性，邏輯清楚。因此閱讀時，可以多觀察文章的整體組織結構，例如：文章共有幾個段落、各段落的論點、主旨在每個段落的發展、句與句之間的邏輯以及轉折詞。閱讀完畢，試著用自己的話重述文章的主旨與主張。這些策略能幫助你掌握敘述者的觀點、態度及寫作目的，也是提升問題理解、思辨分析、推理批判等系統思考素養和解決問題的重要步驟。

   觀察好文章中的連貫性，能幫助自己更快掌握文章主旨與重點，同時也能培養自己成為更好的寫作者。

Note

READING
COMPREHENSION

閱讀測驗

第三部份

閱讀理解

閱讀測驗 第三部份 **閱讀理解**

閱讀理解共 15 題，包含數篇文章，每篇文章會搭配 2-4 個相關的問題。須先理解文章的內容，再根據問題，選出最適合者作答。

> **本部份評量的學習表現包括：**
>
> ✓ 能閱讀不同體裁、主題的文章
> ✓ 能了解文章、書信的內容及文本結構
> ✓ 能熟悉各種閱讀技巧，包括
>   - ★ 擷取大意與關鍵細節
>   - ★ 根據隱含的線索推論
>   - ★ 綜合相關資訊預測可能的發展
>   - ★ 分析、歸納多項訊息的共通點或結論
>   - ★ 分析判斷文章內容，了解敘述者的觀點、態度及寫作目的

考前提醒

這部份評量考生是否具備不同層次的閱讀理解能力。作答時，需善用不同的閱讀策略與系統性思考，以掌握文章的主旨、大意、關鍵細節、了解字裡行間隱含的意義，闡釋作者未於文中直接寫出之訊息、推測作者的言外之意、觀點和態度、與整合歸納文章中的資訊。

這個部份的文章形式有說明文、敘述文、論說文等，體裁則包含廣告、文章、電子郵件、信件、說明書、報章雜誌、圖表、網站資訊等。不同文體的文章，結構和文意鋪陳的方式不太一樣，平時應多接觸各類文體與各式主題文章，答題時才能迅速掌握文章重點。

回答這類型的題目時，你可以

1. 先閱讀題目，適時運用閱讀策略

   閱讀文章前，先瀏覽題目，建立閱讀文章的目標，接著善用閱讀策略（請參考學習策略第一點），優先閱讀答題的關鍵段落，節省答題的時間（例如第 24、27、29、33 題）。

2. 辨識主題句，掌握主旨

   先掌握主題句的句意，可以很快地了解一篇文章的大意。多數文章會在每段第一句提供主題句，概略告訴讀者這段內容的主旨。如果是傳單或圖表的話，要先從標題掌握主旨（例如第 21、32 題）。

3. 詳讀支持句，歸納含意

   一個段落除了開頭的主題句以外，後面還會有數個支持句。顧名思義，支持句的目的是支持主題句，根據文意可分為許多不同功能，例如進一步解釋原因（例如第 25、31題）、說明步驟（例如第 26 題），或是提供細節資訊（例如第 23 題）。有時需要透過內文進一步了解細節資訊或是推論作者的態度及立場，這時就要仔細閱讀文章中的支持句，判斷其與上下文之間的邏輯關係。

4. 熟悉閱讀題型中問題的類型

   閱讀測驗常見的題型有四種，可分為主旨大意題、細節理解題、情境題與推論題：

   (1) 主旨大意題：問文章的主旨、大意或適合的標題，例如第 26 題 What is this article mainly about?（這篇文章主要的內容是？）
   (2) 細節理解題：問文章的重要細節，例如第 28 題 What information is provided in the article?（文章提供下列哪一個資訊？）
   (3) 情境題：問文章出處或是人物的職業、彼此的關係，例如第 23 題 What is true about Martin and Kim's relationship?
       （Martin 和 Kim 的關係為何？）
   (4) 推論題：問作者未於文中直接寫出之訊息、言外之意，考應用所得資訊進行推論，例如第 31 題 If Phil rejects Brandon, what might be the reason?（如果 Phil 拒絕 Brandon，原因可能是什麼？）。

平時閱讀文章時，可以練習試著問自己上述這些問題，一邊讀、一邊整理讀到的資訊，不僅可以提高閱讀速度，還可以更深入的理解文章。

Underwater World

On Fisherman Road next to Civic Harbor

Are you ready for a close encounter with sharks, jellyfish, and giant turtles?

Visit *Underwater World*, home of the nation's largest exhibits of ocean life, and you'll see sea creatures you have never seen before as you walk through our 100-meter-long glass tunnel.

Don't miss our daily seal shows, which start at 11:00 A.M. and 2:00 P.M.

Opening hours:

Monday to Saturday, 10:00 A.M. to 8:00 P.M.

Sunday, 10:00 A.M. to 5:00 P.M.

Entrance fees:

Children aged 6 and under: Free

Students: NT$250

Adults: NT$400

Senior citizens (over 65): NT$200

本篇為一則廣告，內容為「水底世界」水族館的相關營業資訊。

第 21 題

What is this advertisement for? | 這則廣告是關於什麼？

A.　A huge aquarium
B.　A fishing trip
C.　A famous museum
D.　An underground mall

A.　一座大型水族館
B.　一趟釣魚之旅
C.　一間知名的博物館
D.　一家地下商城

正解 Ⓐ

題目問這則是有關什麼的廣告。先閱讀廣告的標題，再找出和標題相關的字詞。

從標題 Underwater World（水底世界）和後文提到的 sharks（鯊魚）、jellyfish（水母）、giant turtles（巨型烏龜），和能走進 tunnel（隧道）觀看 ocean life、sea creatures（海洋生物），還能觀賞 seal shows（海豹表演），即可得知這是水族館刊登的廣告，因此正確答案為 A。

關鍵字詞 underwater 在水中的　sea creature 海洋生物　show 表演

What information can be found in the advertisement?　　廣告中可以找到什麼資訊？

A.　How to make a reservation	A.　如何訂位
B.　What kind of seafood is served	B.　供應哪種海鮮
C.　How long the show will last	C.　表演時間多長
D.　Who needs to pay for a ticket	D.　誰需要買票

正解　D

題目問廣告中提供的訊息。閱讀時，必須留意當中的關鍵資訊，才能正確回答。

廣告的目的在推銷產品吸引顧客，通常會告知門市地點、時間、價錢等。這則水族館的廣告，主打能觀看許多海底生物，同時也公告水族館的開放時間（opening hours）和購票資訊（entrance fee），列出了不同身分類別的票價，因此，答案是 D：誰需要買票。廣告中提到表演秀的開場時間（請看文章標示紅色的文字），但沒有說明時間長短，因此 C 不是正確答案。

關鍵字詞 opening hours 營業時間　entrance fee 門票費用

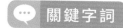 **關鍵字詞**

接著我們來複習本部份的重點詞彙

underwater 形 在水中的（第 21 題）

例句 • Underwater sports like free diving require the technique of holding your breath.
像是自由潛水這類水中運動需要憋氣的技巧。

sea creature 海洋生物（第 21 題）

例句 • You'll see sea creatures you have never seen before as you walk through our 100-meter-long glass tunnel.
當你走進我們長達 100 公尺的海底玻璃隧道時，你會看到從未見過的海洋生物。

• The zoo exhibits several sea creatures like sea turtles and dolphins.
這間動物園展出數種海洋生物，像是海龜和海豚。

show 名 表演（第 21 題）

例句 • Don't miss our daily seal shows, which start at 11:00 A.M. and 2:00 P.M.
別錯過我們的海豹表演，每天上午 11 點與下午 2 點開演。

• An amazing fireworks show was held before the party ended.
派對結束前，有一場精彩的煙火秀。

opening hours 營業時間（第 22 題）

例句 • Due to the coming typhoon, the opening hours of our department store will be shortened today.
由於颱風逐漸逼近，百貨公司今天的營業時間將會縮短。

entrance fee 門票費用（第 22 題）

例句 • The entrance fee to the amusement park is very high. It is suggested to visit it during the off-season when there is a 20% discount.
遊樂園的入場門票相當昂貴。建議淡季時去，會有八折優惠。

From: martinK@netmail.com

To: kph97@mail.com

Subject: Greetings

Dear Kim,

Thank you for the postcard. That was very sweet. I miss you very much, too, and I'm glad to know that your summer job at your uncle's hotel is going well.

Well, my parents finally agreed to let me buy a motorcycle. My dad suggested that I get an electric one and promised to share the cost. After looking at many models, I chose one last week. It's very quiet and makes less pollution than a gasoline-powered one.

Now that I have my own vehicle, I want to visit you. According to my map, Fantasy Lake is only a few miles from your uncle's hotel. I would like to go fishing there and stay at your uncle's hotel for one night. Let me know your days off.

Take care, and write back soon.

Regards,
Martin

本篇為一封電子郵件，內容是 Martin 問候放暑假後未見的朋友 Kim，告知他買了一輛摩托車，並表達想拜訪 Kim 的計畫。

第 23 題

What is true about Martin and Kim's relationship?	Martin 和 Kim 的關係為何？

A. They were schoolmates who founded a club.

A. 他們是創辦一個社團的同學。

B. They are friends who have not met for some time.

B. 他們是一段時間未見的朋友。

C. They are neighbors who are preparing an activity.

C. 他們是在籌備一項活動的鄰居。

D. They were colleagues who worked closely together.

D. 他們是密切合作的同事。

正解 B

題目問寫信人和收件者的關係。答題時先找出信件的基本資訊，包括主旨、寄件人與收件人的姓名，接著略讀每個段落，就能找到正確答案。

從信件主旨 Greetings（問候）可知 Martin 寫信給 Kim 目的是在問候他的近況，且從第一段提到的 I miss you very much.（我很想你）和 your summer job at your uncle's hotel（你在叔叔開的飯店暑期工讀）可得知兩人因為放暑假沒有見面，所以答案是 B：They are friends who have not met for some time.（他們是一段時間未見的朋友）。

關鍵字詞 greeting 問候、招呼　miss 想念、思念

What can be learned about Martin's new motorcycle?

A. It is environmentally friendly.

B. It has a powerful engine.

C. It has a striking appearance.

D. It is custom-made.

下列哪個有關 Martin 新摩托車的描述符合文章內容？

A. 它很環保。

B. 它的引擎很有力。

C. 它的外觀很炫。

D. 它是訂製的。

正解 A

只要讀懂題目所提事物，找出文中形容 new motorcycle（新摩托車）的句子，便可知其特色。

詳讀信件第二段有關摩托車的描述，Martin 提到他的爸爸建議他買電動（electric）車，後面描述這種車的特色為安靜又比較不會造成汙染（make less pollution），因此正確答案是 A：It is environmentally friendly.（它對環境很友善，亦即環保）。信中沒有提及 engine（引擎）或 appearance（外觀），且 Martin 是看了眾多車款後才挑選的（after looking at many models），不是特別訂製的（custom-made），所以 B、C、D 都不是正確答案。

關鍵字詞 pollution 汙染 environmentally friendly 環保

第 25 題

Why does Martin hope to hear from Kim soon?

A. He is seeking employment.

B. He is sending Kim a present.

C. He is asking Kim for help.

D. He is planning a journey.

Martin 為何希望趕快收到 Kim 的回覆？

A. 他正在找工作。

B. 他要寄禮物給 Kim。

C. 他需要 Kim 的幫忙。

D. 他在規劃一趟旅行。

正解 Ⓓ

題目問 Martin 希望 Kim 早點回信的原因。

Martin 在信中第三段一開始便表明 I want to visit you（我想去拜訪你），而且還想去湖邊釣魚（go fishing）並在 Kim 暑期工讀的旅館過一夜（stay at your uncle's hotel for one night），最後請 Kim 告知何時休假（days off）。綜合這些資訊，就知道 Martin 打算造訪 Kim。因此，正確答案是 D：He is planning a journey.（他在規劃一趟旅行）。

關鍵字詞 visit 拜訪　go fishing 釣魚　stay at 在…留宿

接著我們來複習本部份的重點詞彙

greeting 名 問候、招呼（第 23 題）

例句 • I mailed a card and a gift to my homestay family to send my Christmas greetings.
我寄了一張卡片和一份禮物給我的寄宿家庭，傳達我的聖誕祝福。

miss 動 想念、思念（第 23 題）

例句 • I miss you very much, too.
我也非常想念你。

• When studying at a boarding school, the young child missed his parents and cried a lot.
這小孩就讀寄宿學校時，常因想念父母親而哭泣。

pollution 名 汙染（第 24 題）

例句 • The electric motorcycle is very quiet and makes less pollution than a gasoline-powered one.
電動機車非常安靜，而且與燃油機車相比，製造較少的汙染。

• In the city, it's getting more difficult to see stars at night because of light pollution.
由於光害的關係，在城市裡，越來越難在晚上看到星星。

environmentally friendly 環保（第 24 題）

例句 • Taking public transportation to work is environmentally friendly. It produces a lower carbon footprint than riding in private vehicles.
比起駕駛個人交通工具，搭乘大眾運輸去工作較為環保。後者產生的碳足跡較少。

visit 動 拜訪（第 25 題）

例句 • Now that I have my own vehicle, I want to visit you.
　　　現在我有自己的機車，我想去拜訪你。

　　　• I visit my grandparents only twice a year because we do not live close.
　　　我一年只拜訪祖父母兩次，因為我們住得不是很近。

go fishing 釣魚（第 25 題）

例句 • I would like to go fishing there and stay at your uncle's hotel for one night.
　　　我想到那兒釣魚，並在你叔叔的飯店留宿一晚。

　　　• My grandfather used to work as a fisherman, but now he goes fishing as a leisure activity.
　　　我祖父過去捕魚維生，但是現在他把釣魚當作一種休閒活動。

stay at 在…留宿（第 25 題）

例句 • We will stay at a cabin in the mountain since it got dark early due to the storm.
　　　因為暴風雨的關係，天提早暗了，因此我們會待在山中的木屋。

Note

East Asians are familiar with the physical benefits of bathing in hot springs. In Finland, people use saunas for similar reasons. A sauna is a small wooden hut or a room inside a house. By means of a stove, the sauna is first heated to between seventy-one and one hundred degrees Celsius. After people shower and clean themselves, they go into the sauna and sit on a wooden bench. They take a towel with them to sit on, as the bench might be quite hot. Every few minutes, they pour some water over heated stones on top of the stove to create new steam. After a while they go outside, jump into a pond or take a cold shower, and then go back into the sauna again. They repeat this process two or three times and wash themselves again at the end. Afterwards, they enjoy Finnish sausage with beer or soft drinks. Saunas are very popular in Finland, and there are two million saunas for the country's entire population of 5.5 million people.

本篇短文為一敘述文，內容介紹芬蘭人如何洗蒸氣浴，接著描述洗蒸氣浴的步驟。最後，以蒸氣浴在芬蘭受歡迎的程度作為文章總結。

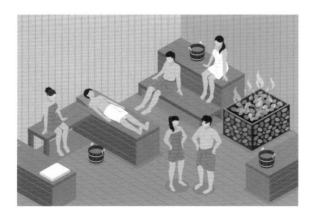

第 26 題

What is this article mainly about?

A. How hot springs and saunas are different

B. Why taking a sauna bath is good for you

C. How people in Finland take a sauna bath

D. Where the best locations for saunas are

這篇文章主要關於什麼？

A. 溫泉和蒸氣浴有何不同

B. 為什麼洗蒸氣浴對你有益處

C. 在芬蘭人們如何洗蒸氣浴

D. 蒸氣浴最棒的地點

正解 C

題目問的是文章大意。

文章提供了幾個重要訊息（請見文章中紅字），像是「準備蒸氣房加熱」、「人們坐在蒸氣房中」、「在蒸氣房中澆水增加蒸氣」、「至室外以冷水淋浴」以及「洗完蒸氣浴後吃點心」。這些資訊是依照「洗蒸氣浴」的時間先後順序介紹，由此可知正確答案為 C：How people in Finland take a sauna bath（在芬蘭人們如何洗蒸氣浴）。

除此之外，作者在文章中使用了常用於說明步驟、順序的轉折詞與副詞，例如 first、after、afterwards 等，也是另一個重要的解題關鍵。

關鍵字詞 Celsius 攝氏（溫度）　stove 火爐　process 過程　afterwards 後來

Why do Finnish people take a towel with them into a sauna?

為什麼芬蘭人要帶毛巾去洗蒸氣浴？

A. To clean their faces when they sweat

A. 流汗時用來擦臉

B. To protect themselves from getting burned

B. 保護他們避免燙傷

C. To wrap their hair after a cold shower

C. 在冷水澡後包他們的頭髮

D. To dry the bench before sitting on it

D. 坐上長椅前先擦乾

正解 B

題目問為什麼芬蘭人要帶毛巾去洗蒸氣浴。先找到 towel 一字出現在文章的哪個句子中，細讀該句的上下文，建立正確情境，有助推論正確答案。

根據文章，蒸氣房需要先加溫至攝氏 71 至 100 度之間，接著芬蘭人洗完澡後會進入加熱後的蒸氣房中坐著，作者說明 They take a towel with them to sit on, as the bench might be quite hot.（他們會帶條毛巾並坐在上面，因為椅凳可能有點燙。）人們帶毛巾是為了坐在上面避免燙傷，而不是拿來擦汗或擦水，因此可以判斷正確答案為 B。

關鍵字詞 as 因為

第 28 題

What information is provided in the article?

A. What people do after taking a sauna bath

B. How many families have their own sauna

C. Where people can find stones for the saunas

D. When saunas were first built in Finland

文章提供下列哪一個資訊？

A. 人們洗蒸氣浴後會做什麼

B. 多少家庭有自己的蒸氣浴

C. 人們可以在哪裡找到蒸氣浴的石頭

D. 芬蘭第一個蒸氣浴建造於何時

正解 A

題目問文章提供了哪一個訊息。

選項 A 為「人們洗蒸氣浴後會做什麼」，文章寫道 Afterwards, they enjoy Finnish sausage with beer or soft drinks.（接著，他們享用芬蘭香腸配啤酒或無酒精飲料。），因此 A 為正確答案。

文章最後雖然有提到芬蘭有兩百萬間蒸氣房，但是這個數據並不是以家庭為單位，因此選項 B 不是正確答案。選項 C 為「在哪裡可以找到石頭」，但文章中只提到石頭是蒸氣房增加蒸氣的方法。選項 D：「芬蘭第一個蒸氣浴建造於何時」未出現在內文中，因此這三個選項都不是正確答案。

關鍵字詞 sausage 香腸　soft drink 無酒精飲料

接著我們來複習本部份的重點詞彙

Celsius 名 攝氏（溫度）（第 26 題）

例句 • By means of a stove, the sauna is first heated to between seventy-one and one hundred degrees Celsius.
利用爐火，蒸氣房會先被加溫至攝氏 71 至 100 度之間。

• People in Taiwan use Celsius rather than Fahrenheit to measure temperature.
在台灣人們使用攝氏來標記溫度，而非華氏。

stove 名 火爐（第 26 題）

例句 • Gently warming on the stove is a pot of pork stew.
一鍋燉豬肉在爐子上文火加熱。

process 名 過程（第 26 題）

例句 • They repeat this process two or three times and wash themselves again at the end.
他們重複這個程序兩到三次，最後再洗一次澡。

• The process of applying to this graduate school is divided into several steps as explained on the website.
如同網頁所示，申請這個研究所的程序分成數個步驟。

afterwards 副 後來（第 26 題）

例句 • Afterwards, they enjoy Finnish sausage with beer or soft drinks.
接著，他們享用芬蘭香腸配啤酒或無酒精飲料。

• He worked as an intern at the video game company; afterwards, he got a full-time position.
他以前在這家電玩公司實習；後來，他得到一個全職的職位。

as **連接** 因為（第 27 題）

例句 • They take a towel with them to sit on, as the bench might be quite hot.
他們會帶條毛巾並坐在上面，因為椅凳可能有點燙。

• As he is allergic to milk, he cannot drink latte.
因為他對牛奶過敏，所以不能喝拿鐵咖啡。

sausage **名** 香腸（第 28 題）

例句 • While sausages are seen on breakfast tables in Germany, they are rarely consumed for the morning meal in Taiwan.
在德國的早餐餐桌上常看得到香腸，但是在台灣早餐很少吃香腸。

soft drink 無酒精飲料（第 28 題）

例句 • My daughter is under eighteen, so please serve her soft drinks only.
我女兒未滿十八歲，所以請給她無酒精飲料就好。

Note

Questions 29-31 are based on the information provided in the following web page and email.

Roommate Wanted

Two English majors at Springfield University are looking for someone to share a comfortable, three-bedroom apartment within easy walking distance of the campus. The room will be vacant after July 25. To sharpen our English skills, we enforce a strict "English only" policy in the house. For this reason, we prefer applicants whose mother tongue is English. We also need someone who can pay rent on time and share the housework. If you are interested, please contact Phil at aming@uni.edu.tw. For pictures of the apartment, click **here**.

From: bsmith@uni.edu.tw

To: aming@uni.edu.tw

Subject: Room for rent

Hi Phil,

I am writing in response to your "Roommate Wanted" post. I'm very interested in this apartment since the location is perfect for me. It's near a night market, and I also study at Springfield University. You stated you prefer native English speakers. I am an exchange student from Australia, and am certain I could help you improve your English. I am an easy-going person, and I like to keep my living space tidy and clean. In your pictures, I saw gym equipment, which would be good for my new workout routine. Your cat also looks very cute! I only have one question. My summer program will start on July 1, so I'd like to know if it's possible for me to move in before then. Looking forward to hearing from you!

Cheers,
Brandon Smith

本篇為一則公告及一封電子郵件，內容是說明一位交換生透過電子郵件回應一則徵室友的公告。

Which aspect of a potential roommate does the notice emphasize?

A. Their major in college

B. Their gender

C. Their hobby

D. Their first language

公告特別強調室友人選的哪一面向？

A. 他們的大學主修

B. 他們的性別

C. 他們的嗜好

D. 他們的母語

正解 D

題目問公告強調「室友」須具備的哪一個條件。答題時，先分辨文中哪一些描述與「公寓」（建築物）有關、哪些和「室友」（人）有關，這麼做可以快速找到關鍵句。

公告寫道 To sharpen our English skills, we enforce a strict "English only" policy in the house. For this reason, we prefer applicants whose mother tongue is English.（為了要增進我們的英語能力，我們在家中只說英文。也因此，我們希望新室友可以是一位英文母語人士。）由此可知，正確答案為 D：Their first language（他們的母語）。

關鍵字詞 mother tongue 母語 potential 可能的

第 30 題

What do we know·about Phil?

A. He hopes to adopt a pet.

B. He goes to the gym every morning.

C. He lives near a night market.

D. He speaks Mandarin with his roommates.

關於 Phil 我們知道什麼？

A. 他希望能領養寵物。

B. 他每天早上都去健身房。

C. 他住在夜市附近。

D. 他與室友用中文溝通。

正解 C

題目問我們已知 Phil 是個怎麼樣的人，需要整合兩個文本的資訊。

從電子郵件的署名可知，Brandon 正在找住處，Phil 是正在找尋新室友的人。想要得到較多與 Phil 有關的線索，必須回到公告內容。公告包含了數個與 Phil 有關的資訊，例如 Phil 和他的室友是 Springfield University 的學生、他們租賃的公寓有三個房間，自公寓可步行抵達校園。此外，Phil 與室友在家裡只說英文，且希望新室友能夠準時付房租並共同維持環境整潔。Brandon 的郵件還提到這間公寓靠近夜市，整合這些線索，再對應題目的四個選項，可知道正確答案為選項 C

If Phil rejects Brandon, what might be the reason?

A. Brandon is difficult to get along with.

B. The rent Brandon suggests is too low.

C. He has nothing in common with Brandon.

D. The date Brandon needs to move in is too early.

如果 Phil 拒絕 Brandon，原因可能是什麼？

A. Brandon 太難相處。

B. Brandon 提議的租金太低。

C. 他與 Brandon 沒有相似之處。

D. Brandon 需要搬進公寓的日期太早。

正解 D

本題跟第 30 題一樣，需要整合歸納這兩篇文本中的訊息，推論 Phil 拒絕 Brandon 的原因。

閱讀時可利用搜尋閱讀（search reading）的技巧，快速找到與題目相關的資訊，再整合相關訊息。Phil 在公告中提到 The room will be vacant after July 25.（房間會在 7 月 25 號之後空出來），這表示新房客 7 月 25 日之後才能搬進去。Brandon 在電子郵件中則說明 My summer program will start on July 1, so I'd like to know if it's possible for me to move in before then.（我的暑期課程會在 7 月 1 日開始，因此我想知道我是否能在那之前就搬進去。），整合這兩項訊息可得知，如果 Phil 拒絕 Brandon，最有可能的原因應該是 Brandon 需要搬進去的日期太早。

Phil 與 Brandon 應該還沒有見過彼此，因此無法判斷兩人是否相處愉快；Brandon 沒有在信件中提出有關租金的訊息；Brandon 提到 I saw gym equipment, which would be good for my new workout routine.（我看到健身設備，很適合我新培養的健身習慣。）可推論 Phil 和 Brandon 可能都喜歡健身，選項 A、B 與 C 都不是正確答案。

關鍵字詞 vacant 空的、未被占用的 gym equipment 健身設備、裝備

💬 關鍵字詞

接著我們來複習本部份的重點詞彙

mother tongue 母語（第 29 題）

例句 • We prefer our roommate to be someone whose mother tongue is English.
我們希望室友可以是一位英文母語人士。

• Much influenced by their mother tongue, non-native English speakers may have difficulty distinguishing the R and L sound.
受到母語的影響，非英語為母語者可能會難以辨別 R 和 L 的發音。

potential 形 可能的（第 29 題）

例句 • A potential buyer of a car would ask very detailed questions about its features, speed, and safety.
車子的潛在買家會問非常細節的問題，關於車子的特色、速度和安全性。

vacant 形 空的、未被占用的（第 31 題）

例句 • The room will be vacant after July 25.
這間房間於七月二十五日之後會空出來。

• The green light on the wall indicates that the restroom is vacant.
牆壁上的綠燈顯示廁所沒人。

gym equipment 健身設備、裝備（第 31 題）

例句 • In your pictures, I saw gym equipment, which would be good for my new workout routine.
我在你的照片上看到健身設備，很適合我新培養的健身習慣。

• The gym equipment over there is under repair, so people are crowded here using the treadmills.
那邊的健身器材維修中，所以人們擠在這邊用跑步機。

In the 1730s, America consisted of thirteen English colonies, one of which was New York. **The governor of New York, William Cosby, was appointed to his position by the English government.** He was widely disliked because of his attempts to raise his salary, seize lands, and even influence the result of a local election.

In 1733, a newspaper published articles that described Cosby's abuses of power. In response, Cosby had the publisher, John Peter Zenger, arrested and put in jail. Zenger was accused of damaging Cosby's reputation by making false statements about him.

Zenger spent eight months in prison before appearing in court. **Two judges and a twelve-man jury listened to the case. Zenger's lawyer admitted that Zenger had printed the articles about Cosby. However, he fiercely defended Zenger's right as a journalist to tell the truth about people even if it disgraced them.**

After discussing the case, the jury ruled in favor of Zenger, saying that he had not committed any crime because what he had published could be proven. **As a result, Zenger was set free. It was the first trial in America that focused on a newspaper's right to publish articles critical of government officials or other people. This ruling helped to establish the principle of freedom of the press, a right that journalists in America and many other countries enjoy today.**

本篇短文為一篇敘事文（narrative），內容講述一位美國報刊發行人 John Peter Zenger 因為出版批判紐約總督 William Cosby 濫權的新聞而歷經牢獄之災，這個事件對於推動美國新聞自由有重要的影響。

第 32 題

What is the main subject of this article?

A. An election with opposing candidates

B. A debate between rival newspapers

C. A false statement about an official

D. A legal case involving a journalist

這篇文章的主題是什麼？

A. 一場候選人立場對立的選舉

B. 一場新聞競爭同業間的辯論

C. 對一位官員的錯誤聲明

D. 一起與新聞工作者有關的司法案件

正解 Ⓓ

題目問的是文章的主旨，掌握文章每個段落的主題句（請見文章紅字），就可以歸納出正確答案。

第一段主題句提供時間背景的線索，在 1730 年代的美國紐約，社會大眾對其總督 William Cosby 充滿負面觀感。第二段主題句告訴我們一間報社出版了一篇文章，批評 Cosby 濫用權力。第三段圍繞在報刊發行人 Zenger 的遭遇與他的律師替他辯護的重點，關鍵字包含 defend（捍衛）、right（權利）和 disgrace（使丟臉）。文章最後一段的主題句 After discussing the case, the jury ruled in favor of Zenger, saying that he had not committed any crime because what he had published could be proven. 講述最終 Zenger 的報導屬實，而獲判無罪的決議。整合這些資訊，可以判斷這篇文章描繪的是 A legal case involving a journalist（一起與新聞工作者有關的司法案件）。

關鍵字詞 abuse 濫用　jury 陪審團　rule 做出裁決　in favor of 支持、有利於

What was the public's opinion of Cosby?

社會大眾對 Cosby 的觀感如何？

A.　His experience was inadequate.

A.　認為他的經驗不足。

B.　He would improve in time.

B.　認為他會逐漸進步。

C.　His conduct was wrong.

C.　認為他的行為有錯。

D.　He deserved a higher salary.

D.　認為他應得更多薪資。

正解 Ⓒ

題目問的是社會大眾對 Cosby 的觀感如何。

這個資訊在文章的第一段：He was widely disliked because of his attempts to raise his salary, seize lands, and even influence the result of a local election.（他不受大眾喜愛，因為他企圖提高自己薪資、奪取土地、甚至介入地方選舉）。由此可知，正確答案應為 C。

關鍵字詞 attempt 企圖、嘗試　seize 奪取、抓住

第 34 題

What was the intention of Cosby's action towards Zenger?

A. To stop attacks against Zenger

B. To persuade Zenger to leave the U.S.

C. To release Zenger from prison

D. To destroy Zenger's career

Cosby 對 Zenger 所做的行為目的為何？

A. 欲遏止針對 Zenger 的攻擊

B. 欲說服 Zenger 離開美國

C. 欲自監獄中釋放 Zenger

D. 欲破壞 Zenger 的事業

正 解 D

題目問 Cosby 對 Zenger 所做的行為目的為何。閱讀時，掌握 Zenger 和 Cosby 在這個事件中的關係，就能理解事件的脈絡，推論出答案。

根據文本，Zenger 是報刊發行人，印刷出版了一則批評 Cosby 的新聞。總督 Cosby 要求逮捕 Zenger，並指控 Zenger 出版不實言論、傷害他的名譽 (In response, Cosby had the publisher, John Peter Zenger, arrested and put in jail. Zenger was accused of damaging Cosby's reputation by making false statements about him.)。由這個資訊推論，如果 Cosby 沒有要求逮捕 Zenger，Zenger 便能夠繼續在報紙中抨擊 Cosby。如果 Cosby 沒有指控 Zenger 傳播不實資訊，大眾便會相信 Zenger 所出版的內容為真。基於 Cosby 的這兩個行為，可以合理推論 Cosby 想破壞 Zenger 的事業，使大家不信任他刊登的內容。

關 鍵 字 詞 in response 回應　publisher 發行人、出版商

What was the final decision about Zenger?

A. His demands were not realistic.

B. He was found innocent.

C. He received a light punishment.

D. His property would be seized.

針對 Zenger 的最後判決為何？

A. 他的要求不切實際。

B. 他獲判無罪。

C. 他受到輕微的刑罰。

D. 他的財產會遭沒收。

正解 **B**

題目問的是針對 Zenger 的最後判決為何。

我們在文章最後一段找到答題關鍵句：After discussing the case, the jury ruled in favor of Zenger, saying that he had not committed any crime because what he had published could be proven.（經過討論後，陪審團判決 Zenger 勝訴，他們認為 Zenger 所刊登的內容可以被證實，因此沒有犯罪的嫌疑）。此處的 **rule in favor of** 語意為「判決⋯勝 / 支持」，意思即為選項 B：He was found innocent.（Zenger 被認為是無罪的）。

關 鍵 字 詞 set free 釋放 innocent 無罪的、清白的

📄 文本分析

這篇文章為一篇敘事文，全文分為四個大段落。主要是關於一個對於推動美國新聞自由的重要事件。

段落	主旨	內容
1	說明事件背景、介紹主要人物	1. 在 1730 年代的美國紐約，社會大眾對紐約總督 William Cosby 充滿負面觀感。 2. Cosby 企圖提高自己薪資、奪取土地、甚至介入地方選舉，種種惡行導致他不受大眾喜愛。
2	Zenger 的報導與引發的效應	1. Zenger 是一位報刊發行人，刊登了一則批評 Cosby 濫用權力的文章。 2. Cosby 要求逮捕 Zenger，並指控 Zenger 出版不實言論、傷害他的名譽。
3	Zenger 的律師在法庭上的辯護	1. Zenger 尚未受審就先在監獄待了八個月。 2. Zenger 的律師承認 Zenger 確實有刊登批評 Cosby 的文章，但強烈捍衛 Zenger 做為新聞工作者報導真相的權利。
4	法院判決與這個事件的意義	1. 陪審團認為 Zenger 的報導屬實，判決他無罪，並釋放他。 2. 這個事件是美國歷史上第一個針對新聞自由的審判。 3. Zenger 的無罪判決奠定了新聞自由，至今美國和其他地區的新聞業者都享有這個重要權益。

接著我們來複習本部份的重點詞彙

abuse **名** 濫用（第 32 題）

例句 • A newspaper published articles that described Cosby's abuses of power.
一家報社刊登了描述 Cosby 濫權的文章。

• Long-term abuse of alcohol can lead to serious health problems.
長期濫用酒精會導致嚴重的健康問題。

jury **名** 陪審團（第 32 題）

例句 • The jury ruled in favor of Zenger, saying that he had not committed any crime because what he had published could be proven.
陪審團判決 Zenger 勝訴，他們認為 Zenger 所刊登的內容可以被證實，因此沒有犯罪的嫌疑。

• The jury was confused about the inconsistent statement from that witness, so the evidence will be re-examined.
陪審團對於這證人前後不一致的證詞感到困惑，所以證據會被重新檢視。

rule **動** 做出裁決（第 32 題）

例句 • The European Union's top court ruled that the technology company won the case.
歐盟的最高法院裁決這家科技公司贏得訴訟。

in favor of 支持、有利於（第 32 題）

例句 • Some teachers are in favor of using games to teach young learners of English.
有些教師贊成用遊戲教導年輕的英文學習者。

attempt 動 企圖、嘗試（第 33 題）

例句
- Cosby was widely disliked because of his attempts to raise his salary, seize lands, and even influence the result of a local election.
  Cosby 不受大眾喜愛，因為他企圖提高自己薪資、奪取土地、甚至介入地方選舉。

- The novelist attempted to send the draft to the editor by Friday, but she did not know how to conclude the story.
  這位小說家試圖在週五前寄送草稿給編輯，但是她想不出如何將故事收尾。

seize 動 奪取、抓住（第 33 題）

例句
- At the film festival, the young director seized the opportunity to ask the senior producer about future cooperation.
  在電影節中，這位年輕導演抓住機會去詢問資深製作人未來合作的機會。

in response 回應（第 34 題）

例句
- A newspaper published articles that described Cosby's abuses of power. In response, Cosby had the publisher, Zenger, arrested and put in jail.
  一家報社刊登了描述 Cosby 濫權的文章。對此回應，Cosby 派人逮捕發行人 Zenger 入獄。

- In response to the fierce protest against the high unemployment rate, the prime minister of Iraq claimed that a reform would be conducted.
  因應高失業率而起的激烈抗爭，伊拉克總理宣告將會改革。

publisher 名 發行人、出版商（第 34 題）

例句
- After e-books became popular, traditional print media publishers faced a decline in business.
  電子書變得受歡迎之後，傳統的平面媒體出版業者面臨生意下滑。

set free 釋放（第 35 題）

例句
- As a result of the final ruling, Zenger was set free.
  最終判決的結果，Zenger 獲釋。

- The bird was set free from the cage, and it flew away immediately.
  鳥從籠子裡被釋放，牠立即飛走。

innocent 形 無罪的、清白的（第 35 題）

例句 • He was found innocent.
他獲判無罪。

• Though the suspect was eventually found innocent, she went through a long and tiring court case.
雖然這名嫌疑犯最終獲判無罪，她經歷了一場又長又累人的訴訟。

Note

延伸思考

讀完文章後，試著回答以下這幾個問題，幫助我們加深對這個議題的了解、啟發更多思考。

1. If you were Zenger, would you publish articles that criticize the authority's abuse of power?

   想像你是 Zenger，你是否也會刊登抨擊當權者濫權的文章呢？

2. Do you find freedom of the press important? What are some advantages or disadvantages of having freedom of the press?

   你認為新聞自由是否重要？新聞自由有什麼好處或壞處呢？

3. These days, fake news is everywhere on the Internet. What are some ways to distinguish real news from fake news?

   近日，假新聞充斥網路，有什麼方法可以分辨新聞真假？

Note

1. 靈活運用常見閱讀策略（略讀、搜尋閱讀、掃讀、精讀）

「略讀」（skimming）是利用文章的標題、各段落開頭、粗體字等，對文章整體架構有概略性了解後，再決定是否進一步閱讀的策略。「搜尋閱讀」（search reading）則是心裡先有閱讀的目標，有目的地搜尋重要的資訊，到文章裡找答案，必要時才進一步精讀。「掃讀」（scanning）是針對鎖定的目標，通常是特定的數字、名字、日期、地點、字詞等，進行掃描式閱讀，略過與鎖定目標無關的內容。「精讀」（careful reading）指的是仔細地閱讀文章中的每一個句子，確認自己了解每個字句的意思後，再往下閱讀。閱讀文學作品時，讀者們通常會採精讀的策略，如此一來才能細細品嘗作家的文采。相反地，如果是需要在短時間內擷取文章主旨與重點，掃讀、略讀和搜尋閱讀等先略過不重要資訊的閱讀策略，效率較高。熟練這些策略有助於提升閱讀速度，強化資訊吸收，為終身閱讀奠定基礎。

2. 練習整合多篇文本的訊息

雙篇閱讀的題型是以兩篇不同體裁的文本呈現，學習者需要整合歸納兩篇文本的內容才能回答問題，這樣的閱讀符合日常與工作中常需針對單一主題進行多文本閱讀的行為。建議學習者平日閱讀時，可主動尋找不同文體的文章，試著整合歸納兩篇文本的相同或相異處，並明確指出推論的依據。其次，由於雙篇閱讀的篇幅稍長，許多剛接觸的學習者深怕遺漏重要資訊，因此花了許多時間逐字逐行讀完，導致題目寫不完；或是仔細讀完一篇後就失去耐心，另一篇草草看過，遇到問題時需要花加倍的時間回去文章找答案。這都是閱讀技巧不純熟和預測能力不足所致。除了加強略讀、搜尋閱讀等技巧的熟練度，更應提升預測問題的精準度。平時閱讀可試著以 5W1H（請參考中級聽力第三部份學習策略第

三點）為基礎，針對文本的主旨和細節列出問題，先推論可能的回答後再回到文章段落精讀、印證答案。這麼做不但能提升整合多篇文章訊息的能力，也能有效縮短回答問題的時間，讓雙篇閱讀不再可怕。

3. 透過「換句話說」和「總結大意」練習檢視理解

你是否曾閱讀完一篇英文文章，卻想不起剛讀過的內容？確認自己理解多少也是很重要的閱讀步驟。可以利用「換句話說」的方式，透過逐句閱讀，把讀到的句子改用自己的話說出來，一邊確認語意是否還是一樣；另一種方式是閱讀完一份篇章，蓋住文章，憑著剛剛理解的印象試著重述概要，例如這篇文章的主題是什麼、作者的論點與理由為何。這兩項練習不但可以增進理解能力，也能夠幫助找出適合自己的閱讀、理解步驟，培養反思與自我精進的核心素養。

4. 保持閱讀習慣，並利用閱讀擴充並深化單字的學習

保持閱讀習慣是強化閱讀理解的重要一環，同時你也可以開始調整閱讀策略，將閱讀視為學習新單字的機會。閱讀文章時，先不求理解每個單字，也不要馬上查閱字典。可以先用螢光筆標記不懂的字，仔細閱讀該字出現的上下文，利用前後語境，宏觀式地理解文章主旨與重要訊息，來推論這些沒看過的字彙可能代表的意思。接著再對照字典的翻譯，確認自己的推論是否有誤。這個方法可以幫助我們在更完整豐富的語境中學習新的字彙與其用法。越來越熟練後，你會發現自己閱讀的速度與效率倍增。

平時可擬定英文閱讀計畫，依照上述閱讀策略的重點，執行並檢討閱讀成效，改善閱讀效率，培養規劃應變的能力與自我精進的核心素養。

全民英檢學習指南—中級聽讀測驗

主　　編：沈冬

編 輯 群：財團法人語言訓練測驗中心（LTTC）

出 版 者：財團法人語言訓練測驗中心（LTTC）

地　　址：10663 臺北市大安區辛亥路二段 170 號

電　　話：（02）2362-6385 傳真：（02）2364-0379

網　　址：www.lttc.ntu.edu.tw

封面設計：恣遊設計有限公司

印　　刷：秋雨創新股份有限公司

出版日期：民國 109 年 3 月初版

定　　價：平裝本新臺幣 380 元

ISBN 978-986-94222-3-9（平裝附光碟片）

全民英檢學習指南 中級聽讀測驗 / 沈冬主編 . -- 初

版 . -- 臺北市 : 語言訓練測驗中心 , 民 109.03

　　冊；　公分

ISBN 978-986-94222-3-9（平裝附光碟片）

1. 英語 2. 讀本

805.1892　　　　　　　　　　109000864